Royal Protection

Royal Protection

An Erotic Collection

A Temptation Press Anthology

Royal Protection

An Erotic Collection

A Temptation Press Anthology

© 2020 Temptation Press, et al.
An Imprint of Zimbell House Publishing
Published in the United States by Temptation Press

This book is rated for 18+

All Rights Reserved

Trade Paper ISBN: 978-1-64390-178-7
.mobi ISBN: 978-1-64390-179-4
ePub ISBN: 978-1-64390-180-0
Library of Congress Control Number: 2020939633

First Edition: July 2020
10 9 8 7 6 5 4 3 2 1

TEMPTATION
PRESS

Acknowledgments

Temptation Press would like to thank all those that contributed to this anthology. We chose to showcase five new voices that best embodied our vision for this anthology.

We would also like to thank all those on our Temptation Press team for all their hard work and dedication to these projects

Contents

Princess Ditka

Wolfgang Domino

Standing before the monstrous castle in the center of the village, I felt intimidated. It'd been a long road training in the military and working hard to get my position. I couldn't wait to be security for the royal family, the Khaimahs. It'd always been the dream.

I had no direct supervisor. There were half a dozen other guards posted about the castle who would tell me everything I needed to know. I found a friend in one of them, Jothat, right before taking the detail.

King Musaf and Queen Myrian didn't give me a warm welcome like I had hoped they would. When introduced, they sort of gave me a smirk and continued on with their day. I got the feeling they'd seen a lot of people come and go. I couldn't help but feel starstruck when I met them. I'd heard about them nearly every day of my life.

"It's an honor to have you aboard," said a loud voice from behind me.

I turned around to see the speaker's face. "Princess Ditka. It's … um. I'm, uh, glad." My face began to get hot as I looked at her. Princess Ditka was the most beautiful woman in the world. I couldn't form a full sentence.

I'd had a thing for Ditka, even though I didn't know her all that well. I would smile upon seeing her face, and occasionally, I would see a portrait of hers in the market. A picture of Ditka went for top dollar. I'd always secretly wanted one, but never went about getting one.

"What my comrade means to say is that it's nice to meet you, Princess Ditka," Jorhat said, speaking for me in what could have been an embarrassing situation.

Long, black hair trailed down the shoulders of Princess Ditka. Beautiful ebony skin seemed to glow. Perfect teeth shone through a beautiful smile. "It's nice to meet you two." Ditka turned to Jorhat and said, "You will be guarding my parents." She then looked at me and said, "You will be guarding me. You do have a name, right?"

"Mendonca."

"Well then, Mendonca, are you prepared to walk beside me while we go to the market?"

I had a feeling she would have gone to the market with or without me. She gave off that vibe. She'd always done what she wanted.

"Yes, of course. I will guard you with my life," I said. *What a stupid thing to say*, I thought.

After the introductions, Jorhat walked into the other room, trailing the king and queen. Ditka and I were alone, which had been my biggest fear. I had to get my tongue out of a knot to speak to her. Of all the things the military had prepared me for, speaking to the princess was not one of them.

"I need to change before we go," she said.

I followed the princess through the long corridors of the castle, watching her every move. Not many threats existed inside the castle. We passed by staff cleaning and working hard at their daily labors. Some of them greeted the princess as she passed by, and she returned the pleasantries, remembering all of their names.

She stopped in front of a massive wooden door. "You can wait right here, Mendonca."

Even the way she said my name made me melt.

The princess opened the door, slid inside, and quickly returned wearing a beautiful orange garb. "Are you ready?" she asked, smiling. The smile could have lit a room.

We walked through the courtyard together and out into the open streets. People who saw her smiled and waved. They looked at me and apprehensively smiled. I could tell by their body language that some of them had shaken her hand and hugged her when there wasn't a bodyguard around. They looked at me questioningly. I wasn't wearing traditional clothes to guard the royal family.

"Ditka, thank God for you and your family," one man cheered from the market.

"You're too kind," she said in return.

Casually walking through the market, looking down at all the trinkets and fresh fruit, Ditka appeared at ease. She didn't think anyone threatened her. She didn't even look over her shoulder. Nothing seemed to bother Ditka, which I admired.

"My father insists I have a bodyguard. Just because he lives in the castle and seldom comes out doesn't mean I'm going to live like that. I like my freedom. I like coming out here and learning the real problems of my country. It's good to talk to some of these people face to face."

The wind blew through her hair. I bit my tongue, trying not to say something stupid.

A child stood at the edge of a table, eyeballing a large bag of candy. Drool practically ran from the little girl's mouth. The man behind the table was working hard, cooking something over an open fire. Ditka took notice of this, and, after getting the man's attention, she pointed to the candy. The man brought over the bag and sold her three pieces.

"Here you are, little lady," Ditka said, leaning down and handing the girl a piece of candy.

"Thank you, Princess." The little girl wrapped her arms around Ditka.

"Please, call me Ditka."

The little girl blushed, popped the candy into her mouth, and walked away. I'd then realized she might hang on to that memory for a long time. It could be the talk of her whole day. Something so small could ripple into something much bigger. I imagined the little girl telling her friends or family that she'd gotten a piece of candy from the princess.

"Mendonca," the princess said, holding out a piece for me.

"Thank you," I said, taking the candy and unwrapping it. I took it in a bite. It was soft, sweet, and perfect, just like Ditka.

"You're welcome," she said, smiling. Ditka unwrapped her candy while strolling along and observing the market. "I would like to buy some fish," she said.

"Fish?" I asked. "Couldn't you just ask the staff to go out and get it for you?"

"We're already out, and besides, I don't like them cooking for me every day. I am capable of cooking for myself."

The look on her face made me question my words. "I didn't … I mean—"

"Relax, Mendonca. I was messing with you. What do you say? Do you like fish?"

"Sure."

We carried on down the stone path, looking left and right at all the tents, which consisted of everything imaginable. If I'd had some free time, I would have considered buying a few things. I didn't get this close to the market often. I lived in the country, far away from the market.

The hum of the market felt settling. At no point did I feel as if there were an immediate threat. Ditka walked through like she'd been there a hundred times before, without a single thought of security. The locals seemed to receive her well. Some of them whispered and pointed, but they all seemed to be smiling.

A man stood under a tent. I knew him to be a fish vendor long before we got there because of the smell.

Ditka walked to the shelter and looked at all the fish displayed on the ice. "They all look so good. Great catch, boys," she said.

"Thank you, Princess Ditka," they said in return.

She looked at all the offerings carefully, thinking deeply about which one she might choose. "This one," she said as she pointed to a large fish.

The man offered her a good deal, but she refused. She insisted on paying the full price.

"I don't want any special treatment," she said.

He wrapped the fish tightly in a bag and handed it to her, thanking her profusely for her business. The men looked genuinely happy to have seen her.

As we walked away, she explained, "We have the money to buy the fish. By buying locally, the money goes back into the community. We could have fish delivered in bulk to the castle, but the money wouldn't get dispersed here. It would all go to a company with no soul."

I guess I hadn't thought that deeply about the economics of the village. The strong scent of fresh bread wafted through the air as we walked. Ditka would do a great job running the country. Of that, I didn't have a single doubt.

"It's amazing down here," Ditka said. "My father forbade me to come here as a child. He said it was too dangerous. I said, 'If you run your country to the best of your ability, you should never be afraid.'" A sneaky smile appeared on her face. "Besides, his words didn't stop me from coming down here."

She had a good point, but we couldn't take the chance. Although a peaceful village now, Massatook had seen violence in the past. There'd been treaties with all of the local enemies, but we could never be too careful.

Two children ran through the marketplace, one chasing after the other. Their laughter bellowed as they ran through, nearly knocking over a woman carrying a basket on her head.

"Mendonca, do you think I will make a good queen? The time is coming." Her voice had this soft sincerity.

"Yes, of course you will, Ditka. You will make a fine queen."

"Do you truly believe that?" Her eyes nervously met mine.

"I wouldn't say it if it wasn't true."

Ditka took my hand in hers and kissed the back of it. "You're a good man, Mendonca."

A thrill set inside of me as her soft lips touched the back of my hand. I couldn't imagine what it would be like to feel them pressed against mine. I wanted to know in the worst way. I'd been thinking about her in such a fashion all day. It would be too much risk to get involved. Besides, I knew she'd never get with the likes of me. She was a princess who had the landscape of any man she pleased. She could marry into money. Why would she look at me, a royal guard?

For a second, we stared into each other's eyes, my hand still in hers. I saw something there. In Ditka's brown eyes, I saw the future … the two of us. I tried to shake the thoughts off, but I couldn't. Lust enticed me, and I took her hand to my lips as well.

"Oh, Mendonca," she whispered, biting her lip. She reached out, grabbed my arm, and smiled. "You're a strong man. I feel so comfortable in your care ... so safe."

We walked back toward the castle, hoping nobody had paid much attention to our endeavor. If someone caught wind of our interaction, it could be the rumor of the village. Someone might start saying that Ditka slept with her guards, to which her father might not take kindly. He didn't, however, have much say, considering she was of the age to marry and would soon run the kingdom herself.

Saying goodbye to Ditka for the night proved to be challenging. I didn't want to take my eyes off her, but I did. I bid her farewell and went home. On my journey home, I thought about her often. Ditka was sexy as hell, witty, and everything I wanted in a wife. Guarding her seemed harder and harder to do. I figured I'd become too distracted with such thoughts of her.

At home, I slept alone, enchanted with a single dream of her. Ditka and I were having furious, passionate sex within the confines of the castle. She'd climbed on top of me and rode me as hard as she could, moaning and groaning. Everything felt real. I could smell her hair and feel her nails as they caressed my chest. The taste of her skin lingered on my tongue. I was disappointed when I awoke and discovered it to be only a dream.

The thought resonated in the back of my mind. I couldn't help revisiting the dream throughout the morning as I ate and gathered my things for another day. I couldn't wait to see Ditka. If she knew such fantasies passed through my mind, would she be interested? I'd thought for a second that I'd seen something in her eyes, maybe even desire?

The sun crept over the marketplace as I walked through. The tents were still there, but not all of the products had arrived yet. People were shuffling in, carrying their items. The market came to life before my eyes. It didn't move with the same busy pace it did during midday, but people were coming to life. The children of the vendors were rubbing crust from their eyes, not quite ready to run and gallivant.

The guard at the gate saw me coming, smiled, and asked me for my information. I told him about the security detail and showed him my credentials. He looked them over carefully.

"You're guarding Ditka?" he asked, giving me the eye.

"Yes."

"Lucky. A friend of mine is right in love with her, but she won't give him the time of day."

I didn't know why he'd tell me this information, but it made me laugh. Ditka's love life often became rumors for the village. People would speculate about whether she had a boyfriend.

Upon my entrance into the castle, I saw some of the other guards. Some of them looked familiar, and others did not.

The king walked by me, yawning deeply, a glass of milk held loosely in his hand. "Another beautiful day," he said sarcastically, sitting down at a nearby table.

The queen walked inside the room and sat down at the table beside her husband. "Ditka should be down at any moment for breakfast."

The staff raced about, setting plates of hot food in front of them. The utensils and such clashed around as everyone moved as swiftly as they could in the morning chaos. The strong scent of coffee lingered in the air.

"We shall find her a suitable husband," the queen said. "Then, we can retire and travel as you've always wanted."

"It would be nice to get away for a bit," he grumbled. "I haven't met a man worthy of my daughter's hand in marriage," he added.

"She is your little girl, and I don't think you will ever think of someone as worthy," she replied, lifting coffee to her lips.

I am worthy, I thought. *I could make an excellent husband for Ditka.* The dream seemed unreasonable and farfetched. I momentarily imagined what it would be like to be married to her. It seemed like it would be a good life. Perhaps I was biased, but I thought we were right for each other.

"Would you be a dear and fetch Ditka for us?" the queen asked me.

Without delay, I walked out of the kitchen and down the hall. The long corridors of the castle reminded me of something from a fairytale. Torches and pictures of ancestors lined the hallways. I couldn't believe how big the building was, even on my second day inside.

I remembered which room belonged to the princess from the day before. The hollow sound of my knock seemed to echo through the long hall.

"Come in," Ditka said.

I walked into the room and found Ditka lying in the bathtub. "Oh, I'm sorry," I said. I stepped away, making an honest effort to cover my eyes and retain her privacy.

"Don't be. I am not ashamed of my body," Ditka said.

From my position, I couldn't see much of anything. The walls of the tub sat too high to expose any nudity.

"Your family is expecting you at the breakfast table."

"Can you be a doll and fetch me that towel?"

I walked further into the room, looked left, and looked right. I hadn't been inside the place before. The bathroom extended from the bedroom, and both were large. I fetched the towel and reached out to hand it to her. I tried to be polite and turn away, but she grabbed my hand. The warm water dripped from her hand and my arm.

"Don't go," she whispered. She lifted herself from the tub, bubbles falling off her tight, sexy body. She took my hand and placed it on her chest.

"Oh my," I whispered.

The firm feeling of her breast in my hand brought on an immediate reaction below. She took her hand off mine, allowing me the freedom to roam. My hand slid across her smooth skin, feeling her breasts. I couldn't help myself as I stared down at them in shock and awe. I'd never expected Ditka to make a move on me. I pinched her nipple with two fingers.

"Like what you see?" she asked.

"Yes."

"I've been in here teasing myself … thinking about you." She stepped out of the tub, dripping water on the floor and wrapping herself in the towel. She looked terrific wet. Her beautiful hair clung to her naked body. "I want you, Mendonca." Ditka rubbed the towel across her body, quickly drying herself off. She dropped the towel.

My arms enveloped around her thin body. My hands fell from her back to her ass and cupped both cheeks. They felt terrific, beautiful, and firm. We kissed, exchanging long, passionate kisses. Her embrace, although slightly wet, felt great. Her nipples poked against my skin. We kissed again, lightly pecking each other's lips. Ditka's thick lips felt incredible and sweet against mine, and it was everything I imagined.

Her cold hand reached down and grabbed the front of my pants. It wasn't long before she'd shimmied them to the floor. On her knees, looking up at me, Ditka took me into her mouth. The pressure of her hand and the feel of her soft lips made me tremble. Her head rocked back and forth, taking me deeper and deeper. The princess worked hard on me. Her head bobbed, and her hand cupped my balls as she worked the shaft with her wet, shiny lips. I took her head, guiding it with my hand.

She stopped and pointed to the bed. Eager, I ran across the room and jumped up on the bed. My shirt flew off my back and landed on the floor. My pants remained in the bathroom. As if she knew I'd be watching, Ditka ambled toward the bed, strutting. Her thighs moved in perfect sequence as she walked across the room.

I took her in, looking at her slim figure. She looked amazing, a sight to behold. She had giant boobs and nice, black legs with finely-trimmed pubes. Her saunter enticed me. Suddenly, I found myself holding my breath.

Ditka planted a hand on my chest, pushing me down flat against the bed. She climbed on top of me, her hair dripping cold water onto my chest. Her soft hands raced up and down my core, rubbing passionately. She leaned down, biting my lip.

"I've wanted this since we met," she whispered.

Her cold hand took my erection and slid it inside. She hadn't been lying about wanting it. Her body pulsed on mine as she moved. The way she gyrated her hips brought me immense pleasure unlike any woman ever had before.

On top of me, she moaned, thrashing her body about in passion. I felt blessed just to witness such a thing. I'd been astounded by her sexual freedom. Ditka groaned, biting and clawing at me like a piece of meat. Her beautiful brown nipple slid into my mouth. Her sexual confidence kept me entranced. There is something so hot about a woman who knows what she wants in the bedroom and isn't afraid to take it. She rode on top of me, arching her back, breasts in the air. The subtle moans set fires inside me as I yearned for more.

We were in the throughs of passion when a knock came from the door. Both of us froze, staring at each other in confusion. I'd forgotten to fetch Ditka for breakfast.

"You should hide," she said. "If they find out I am sleeping with my guard, you will be fired."

I slid off the bed and quickly stowed away under it.

Her mother walked through the door. Ditka slid under the blankets just in the nick of time.

"Are you feeling all right, dear?" she asked, walking into the room.

"No. I sent my guard off to collect some ginger root and berries from the market. I don't think I will be able to do much today," she said. She faked a couple of coughs. Ditka snuggled under the blanket, hiding her nakedness from her mother.

Her mother sat down on the edge of the bed and looked at her for a second. She pressed a hand against her forehead to see if she had a temperature. She didn't.

"The ceremony for you to select your husband is coming up. You should be excited about that," the queen said, testing the water on the topic. "I know having your father select your choices for your husband seems odd, but he is looking out for your best interests."

"It's not fair," Ditka muttered.

The queen kissed her forehead and waltzed out of the room. She could be heard humming as she walked down the long corridor. When the humming dissipated, I came up from under the bed.

"That was close," Ditka said with a laugh. "I suggest you actually go to the market and get those things. It will be more believable if you have them. Get out of the castle unseen."

Sneaking past the king and queen proved to be simple. They were still in the kitchen, discussing Ditka's marriage. The king had been talking about a man he'd met in the village who was a little older than her, but a standup guy.

I slid out of the castle, smiled at the guard outside, and walked down to the market. I collected the berries, but the ginger root proved hard to find. It took me three tables and plenty of wandering to find it. I'd never known what it looked like before.

The two children played in the marketplace, running up and down the tight aisles. It reminded me of the time Ditka bought that little girl candy. She'd been so happy. For the third or fourth time that day, I considered becoming the husband they'd all been searching for. The royal family didn't know me all that well since I'd only worked there for a few days, but I wanted to marry Ditka in the most serious way.

I returned with the ginger root and berries. Ditka lay on the bed, scantily dressed in nightwear. Those seductive eyes watched me. I could feel myself stiffening again under my clothes. We were preparing for another round.

"What do you say we give it another try?" she asked.

"You're the princess," I said with a laugh.

I placed the stuff down on a nearby table and pounced across the floor, pushing her back onto the bed. Passionately, desperately, I kissed her. My tongue slid into her mouth, and I felt the wetness of her kiss. Her robe didn't stay on long. It landed on the floor as I grasped at her plump breasts.

"Oh, Mendonca." She shuddered under my touch.

I slid down into the crevice of her legs, taking her flower into my mouth. She purred like a wildcat and bucked wildly. I clutched her legs, trying to keep her from climbing up the wall as I ate her peach. The sweet juice drove me wild. The constant lick and rub of her clit made her moan.

I considered that we might need to keep it down to avoid bringing attention to ourselves. We'd almost been caught once, but it didn't stop us from doing it again. Although both of us were in our twenties, we felt like horny teenagers again.

We rolled over, facing the wall, and I slid in from behind. Tight and wet, she felt so good. I couldn't believe I was having sex with her *again*. My ability to control myself disappeared. I slammed into her hard, mashing my hips into her. Ditka moaned and didn't seem to mind that it would be fast.

She leaned back, arching her back, and I snagged a handful of her hair. I laced it through my fingers and pulled tightly, which she seemed to enjoy.

"Oh fuck," she whispered.

I tugged on her hair. The slapping of our bodies clashing together made me harder. The wet, sloshing sound drove me wild.

The princess then climbed on top of me, riding me like a beast. Her body felt great against me, her soft skin caressing mine. When she orgasmed, I felt her shaking knees. Her pussy contracted around me.

Immediately after, she slumped off onto the bed. She took me into her mouth again. "Your turn," she said. Passionately, she sucked, shoving it deep into her throat.

My head leaned back, and I stared at the ceiling as she pulsed against me. The suction felt amazing, and I knew it wouldn't take long. Three or four powerful minutes was all it took. I blew my load, which she swallowed.

We lay naked together for nearly an hour before dressing. Nobody in the castle would be looking for me. If anything, they'd think I'd gone home for the day. We spooned, lying together and holding each other.

"I want to be the one to marry you," I said to Ditka.

"It's funny you should say that, because you're the one I wanted to choose."

"My name isn't even an option."

At this, she smiled and traced a finger down my arm. "It will be," she said. "Even if I have to forge it."

The following morning, people filled the throne room. Ditka stood in front of the crowd, staring out at the audience, the king and queen behind her. Everyone seemed to be eager to hear who she would marry.

"Everyone, can I have your attention?" Ditka spoke to the room, which had been loud with chatter.

The room fell silent.

"My father and I have been talking for quite some time now, and we have decided who will take my hand in marriage."

Her father barely knew I existed. I couldn't imagine he would have signed off on the idea, not without some trickery on her part. I swallowed hard, my nerves on fire. I hadn't been that nervous in some time.

"My husband will be Mendonca."

The people in the crowd looked around at each other, confused as to who that might be.

"Come up here," she said. "He has been my guard, and he is the gentlest person I know."

The room remained quiet as I walked to the front and stood beside Ditka. The people looked at me, trying to determine if they knew me or not. I paid them no mind. Pride filled me. I couldn't believe I would be marrying the woman of my dreams. I'd known of her for a long time. I'd lived in the village for my entire life and had heard about the royal family from birth.

"My father came around," she whispered to me.

She took my hand, and the group in front of us began to clap and cheer. I felt as one for the first time in a long time. Chills ran up and down my spine. I couldn't fight off the smile that covered my face. I couldn't wait to wed.

Ditka and I walked around the crowd, answering questions. It hadn't been a long affair, but I knew exactly what I wanted. We both did.

The king came over and put his hand on my shoulder. I expected him to say something threatening about hurting his daughter, but he didn't. He told me he would be glad to have me in the family, which I thought was interesting.

Royally Fiesty

Shanjida Nusrath Ali

CHAPTER 1

"I said no!" I nearly yell, slapping my palms against the wooden desk.

"Be quiet, Emma. Don't you dare disobey your own father."

"Father, this is unnecessary. We barely know each other. How can I stay with him?"

"You are engaged. It's perfectly reasonable. You. Will. Stay. In. His. House." My father's jaw clenches as he tries to control his anger.

"What about your bodyguards? They can do the job."

He rolls his eyes with a huff like he can't take this anymore. "They are only assigned to me. You know the crisis our country is going through, and now this … You will be safer at his place than here. You will do as you are told."

I lick my dry lips. "He is okay with it? What about his parents?"

"They will be out of the country for meetings over the next few weeks. He was the one who suggested this idea."

That bastard. "But—"

"You are dismissed. Start packing," my father retorts with a stern look, turning his back on me as he looks at the sun setting on the horizon.

I stand as still as a statue for a few moments, hoping that he will change his mind, but sometimes I forget how stubborn the king of Nashville can be.

Clenching my jaw, I stomp back to my room and slam my door with a loud *bang* that must echo throughout the whole palace. I don't care if it's not ladylike behavior.

It's been a year since Mom died, yet Father still hasn't changed. He was cold and stubborn then, and he is cold and stubborn now. Looking at my life from the outside, others undoubtedly think my life is filled with luxury. I must have no problems or worries. I have everything.

They are wrong. I have everything, but I still have nothing. My life has always been controlled by my father. I don't have happiness. I don't have freedom. I don't have a choice. Sometimes I wonder why I was even born into a royal family.

Now this too? I am being forced to move to my fiancé's house—no, sorry, not a house—another *palace*. I have never met the guy, and yet, we will be getting married in two months.

Shedding my Chanel dress, I change into my nightgown and flop down onto my queen-sized bed. I look up at the grand ceiling as I lie down in my vast bedroom.

My biggest surprise was the day when my father told me that Prince Benjamin was going to be my husband. Our marriage was arranged by our fathers when we were kids. I mean, who even does that in the twentieth century?

It's no wonder Father made me go to an all-girl school and college to complete my studies. I was only allowed to go to royal functions and have friends who belonged to a royal bloodline.

Now, with this whole marriage … I feel so suffocated with every passing day that I have no clue how to cope with all this. It's not like I don't ever want to get married, but I want to be with someone who will make me feel … alive. I want someone who will take me to places that I have never seen before … someone feisty … someone dominant. I know I definitely won't find anyone like that in this royal world. Every guy I have met is set on being the next king of his country. It's as if they have never thought or tried to live their lives differently for a moment. It seems like the man I dream of having as my husband only exists in the novels I usually read.

I know my father very well; no matter how many times I say no, he will send me to Prince Benjamin's palace. I swear to get on the prince's nerves until he decides that he doesn't want to marry me. Staying in his palace is the only choice I have left. It's a necessity. My life is in danger, and only Prince Benjamin can save me.

CHAPTER 2

"Are we there yet?" I ask my driver for the millionth time as we head to the Braswell Residence.

"Yes, Princess. We are close to the gateway," Lucas replies with a neutral tone.

My heart speeds up the minute I hear his response. This is actually happening. I'm meeting my future husband, and I'm going to stay at his house.

I even searched for him online to see what he is like. Weirdly, there are zero pictures of him. It's as if his photos are banned from the internet. I checked social media, but that also gave me nothing. Don't judge me. Any normal girl would do the same if she hadn't met her future husband yet. You have to be prepared. All I know about is his family history, net worth, and properties ... all the boring stuff.

I rest my head against the seat as the limo passes through the gateway. The car turns, and the palace comes into view. Any other girl's jaw would drop open in surprise, but I've been living this life since the day I was born. These great foundations and fancy historical interiors fail to grab my attention.

The limo halts in the driveway, and a guard approaches. He opens the door for me like a gentleman, but I know the poor guy has to do it because it's his job. I smooth my white shirt and black pants before exiting the car. I notice the servants already taking my bags and luggage out of the back. Audis and Aston Martins line either side of the entrance. *Showoff.*

Just then, I hear the front door of the palace opening, and the man I see striding toward me takes my breath away. My eyes nearly pop out of my head. The guy is drop-dead gorgeous. He is taller than me; I'm sure I would barely reach his chin. His dark, sexy, black hair is perfectly styled. He has olive skin with a carved jawline. Even his five o'clock shadow makes him look sexier. I have seen men in tailored suits before, but *him* ... my God. He looks like he came from a *GQ* magazine photoshoot and didn't require any Photoshop. The closer he gets, the more I want to keep looking at him.

He finally stands in front of me with a grin before taking my right hand and planting a kiss on it. I feel the tip of his tongue darting out to give my hand a swift caress. That one little touch sets my entire body on fire.

I gulp, feeling my throat becoming dry. *Get a grip, Emma. Be calm. Don't ruin this.*

"Greetings, Princess. I hope your journey went well," he says in his deep, throaty voice.

Dear Lord, even his voice is perfect. Clearing my throat, I answer him. "Thank you. It was fine. Where is Prince Benjamin? Is he too busy with his meetings to welcome me personally?"

He lets out a soft chuckle like I cracked a joke. I frown in confusion.

"What's so funny?" I ask.

"The king wasn't joking when he said you hadn't seen your fiancé before; otherwise, you wouldn't be asking him this question."

Wait. What?

As if reading my unuttered question, he answers me. "I am Prince Benjamin. Believe me when I say that I'm willing to give up any meeting just to get a glance at a beauty like you."

Oh. My. God.

A wide, gloating smile spreads across his face. He squeezes my hand gently, pulling me closer to him, and I end up in his arms.

Feeling nervous, I look around for any of his servants watching us. I am relieved to see that, apart from the guards lingering at every corner, we are the only ones outside.

"Do you greet every princess this way?"

"You are the very first and last." His hands go around my waist, giving it a gentle squeeze while his intense eyes never leave mine.

Gathering my courage, I push him away and smooth out my dress. "We are not married yet, so you aren't allowed to touch me this way. I'm here because I had no other choice, thanks to you. As long as I'm here, you can keep your hands to yourself."

His eyes gleam with amusement and challenge. "Absolutely understandable, Princess." He leans in to whisper into my ear. "But when you plead for my touch and beg to be fucked like my queen, that time, I won't keep my hands to myself."

I gasp. My entire face burns bright red from his dirty words. I should tell him it's wrong and absolutely inappropriate, but his words do the opposite of that. Instead, I feel my nerves racing, my heart skyrocketing, and my breathing getting heavier as I feel desire blooming inside me.

With a wicked smile, he leans back. "Let's get you settled, Princess."

Releasing a heavy sigh, I follow him inside his palace, and he leads me to my bedroom.

It's similar to my bedroom at home, but it is more spacious. My clothes have already been put away in the closet. After checking the bathroom and seeing that my bath products have all been set up, I find Prince Benjamin leaning against the door. I thought he would have left by now.

"Thank you for arranging all of these. You may now leave; I need some rest."

He licks his lips before striding toward me with his hands in his pockets.

God, I want to taste those lips.

"I must say, not even ten minutes have passed by, and I'm already falling under your spell."

I roll my eyes, crossing my arms against my chest. His eyes immediately drop down to my breasts, which are slightly pushed up now. I clear my throat to get his attention, but he looks up with a mischievous smile like he wasn't sorry at all for looking down at my breasts.

"I must say you are far from being a gentleman. The title of *shameless* would suit you more," I retort.

"If admiring such beauty will label me as shameless, then so be it. I would be honored."

Why are his sweet words as sexy as his dirty talking? I'm here to get on his nerves, but he is turning the tables by getting under my skin.

With a grin, he turns and leaves the room before informing me about when dinner is served. "I like you this way," he says over his shoulder, halting near the exit.

"What way?" I ask.

"Royally feisty."

CHAPTER 3

A week passes by in a blink of an eye. A week of spending most of my time either roaming around the palace or reading in the library. A week with no clue about who is trying to harm me.

It started with threatening notes my father received. Later, it moved to photographs sent to me in an envelope. A rush of fear had coursed through my body when I saw pictures of me at the ball, in my college classes, and even in my bedroom. Suspecting the intruder must be from the house, Father fired my bodyguards, leaving me no choice but to come here.

Feeling bored, I decide to have a tour of the prince's bedroom. At dinnertime that first day, he made it clear that I was to steer clear from his bedroom, as he liked to maintain his privacy. I am going to be his wife, so eventually, I will be living in his bedroom. Why wouldn't I be allowed in there? Curiosity gets the best of me, and I decide to sneak into his room while he is out for a charity ball. Tip-toeing down the hallway, I walk swiftly to his bedroom door. Luckily, it isn't locked, so I trespass into his massive bedroom.

King-sized bed. Floor-to-ceiling windows. An entire wall-length wardrobe. Abstract paintings hanging against royal, maroon-painted walls. *Yep. Just like I guessed.*

I survey the room as I walk inside. Walking toward his bed, I skim my hands over the smooth silk bedsheet. Looking around, I stalk toward the open closet, which is lined with suits and business shirts. There is an entire row of expensive polished shoes.

I graze my fingers over the shirts as I look around. His watches are displayed inside a glass drawer, and his ties are all rolled up like they belong in a luxury boutique. Then, a small drawer catches my eye. I notice that it's the only drawer that's closed. My heart suddenly starts beating faster as I move to open it. Surprisingly, it opens easily, and inside, I find a silver key. *What room key is this?* I am examining it when someone clearing his throat makes me jump in surprise.

Turning around, I find Prince Benjamin standing in the doorway with his hands inside his pockets. I flush in embarrassment as if I've been caught stealing. I swallow the lump in my throat as I fiddle with the key in my hand. *Shit.* His expression isn't giving anything away. *Is he angry? Furious? Shit, is he going to tell Father and break off the—*

Hold on. This is my chance. Maybe trespassing in his room will make him see how disobedient I am and what an unsuitable wife I will be. He may actually break off the engagement. With a new purpose, I bury the guilt and embarrassment and stand straight with my head held high.

"I thought I told you not to come to my bedroom," he mutters in his deep, thick voice.

Why does he have to be so hot? "I was bored."

His eyebrow raises before he walks toward me. With each step he takes, my nerves race faster and faster until he is standing in front of me, so close that we are just a few centimeters apart.

"Didn't know boredom would lead you to my room."

"I'm not much of a rule follower."

He sneers. "That I can see clearly. Why were you snooping?"

"I wasn't. I was just looking at your collection. After all, we will share this wardrobe after we get married."

"Oh. What's your excuse for having my key in your hand then?" He nods to my hand, which is still grasping his key.

"I was just curious as to what room this is for."

"You don't want to know."

I cross my arms. "Now I really want to know."

"Trust me, you don't. It's not your thing."

"As your fiancée, I deserve to know what it is. Alternatively, I could ask your mother about it."

An amused smile spreads on his face as he shakes his head. He sighs, licking his lips.

God. He has to stop doing that.

"Okay. I will show you what room this key belongs to, but in return, *I* want something," he whispers.

I narrow my eyes. "What makes you think I'll listen to your demands?"

"I'm pretty sure your father won't be too happy to hear about your snooping tendencies."

Bloody hell. Now he is blackmailing me. Rolling my eyes, I answer. "Fine. What do you want?"

"A kiss."

"What?" I take a step back, my back hitting the closet door.

"A kiss. On my lips. Right here and right now." He leans closer, his breath brushing my cheeks.

I gulp. "But I've never kissed anyone …" I say, my voice trailing off.

"In that case, I'll be happy to be your first, because neither of us is going to leave this room until I get what I want." He puts both his hands on either side of mine, caging me in. "And I always get what I want," he rasps, his lips brushing my cheek with a kiss as light as a feather.

I gasp while biting my lip. I feel goosebumps scattering all over my skin.

"Just one kiss, and then I'll show you where this key will take you."

I watch his pupils dilate. His eyes darken with desire and intensity, pulling me close to him like a magnet. He leans in closer until I feel his lips hovering over mine, making me close my eyes in response. My lips quiver, begging for his touch, for his kiss.

Before I know what's happening, I'm leaning forward, my lips crashing against his in a deep, passionate kiss.

CHAPTER 4

Pushing me against the door, he lunges at me. Both his hands hold my face as he devours me.

This is my first kiss, and I never imagined it to be like this. A soft and gentle kiss? Yeah, I thought that much. But rough and dominating? Never in a million years.

My tongue tentatively strokes his, tracing his lips gently. Grasping my chin with one hand, he takes both my hands in another, placing them above my head. I am helpless with my hands bound, my face held tightly, and my body held hostage. I feel like I'm bound only by him.

He takes full advantage, his tongue exploring my mouth, nibbling my bottom lip every now and then. It's clear how much he wants me … and how much he *needs* me. I'm starting to crave for him as well. It's like nothing else matters.

"You taste like sin, Princess. It's a sin I'm willing to commit every single time I lay my eyes on you," he murmurs between his kisses.

The hand that was grasping my chin starts moving down, tracing my neck before traveling down my breasts. Goosebumps scatter over every inch of my body, making my nerves shiver. I need him. *Now.*

I try to loosen my arms to wrap them around his neck and feel him closer to me, but he tightens his grip, keeping me captive. I can feel desire pooling deep down, making my legs quiver.

"Does the princess need something?" he asks, moving back a bit.

I lean forward to kiss him again, but he leans back with a *tsk.*

"My house, my rules. Answer the question."

I breathe heavily while licking my lips. "I think we agreed on just a kiss."

"That we did … but it seems like you want more. Am I right?" he whispers close against my cheek, curling his fingers around my neck. His hot breath tickles my skin as I close my eyes and whimper for his touch.

"Just say what you need, and you shall have it, Princess."

I gulp. "I … I want you," I whisper, mustering up my courage.

"How badly do you want me?" he asks.

"So badly. I need you so badly."

"Then your wish will be granted, Princess. But …" he says, his voice trailing off. He suddenly moves back, and his touch is gone in an instant.

I frown in confusion. Why did he stop? "But what?"

"Not now. Tomorrow night after the gala," he mutters, a grin spreading across his lips.

"Why not now? What gala?"

"Tomorrow, we will both be attending a gala hosted by the King of San West. You will get your wish tomorrow. Tonight, you will refrain from it as a punishment."

"Punishment?"

He nods. "Yes. For trespassing and going against what I said. You also won't touch yourself either; otherwise, I'll be forced to extend the punishment." He leans in a bit, tracing my cheek with his index finger. "We both know you wouldn't want that." With a quick peck, he leaves the room while I stand there, dumbfounded.

Although he is gone, I can still feel the desire coursing through me. It's like he has turned on a switch that only he can control, whether he is here or not.

If he thinks he can keep torturing me like this, then he has bigger things coming his way. I will make him beg for me. I will torture him until he is crazed by desire.

You want to play? Then let's play, Prince. Game on.

CHAPTER 5

It's almost time for the gala. My dress is hanging in the closet with boxes of matching shoes and jewelry, and a mask rests on top of the dressing table.

I had picked out a sexy, black V-neck gown. Not only is it backless, but it even has a slit. Father will also be at the party, which he told me about after our visit today. He might get pissed off about my revealing dress, but tonight, it's all about playing games.

Prince Benjamin is right across the hall, also getting ready, while I stand in front of the floor-length mirror wearing black lace panties and matching bra with garter belts and thigh-high stockings. The moment I'm about to put on my dress, I hear a soft knock.

"Who is it?" I ask over my shoulder.

I hear his raspy voice on the other side of the door. "It's your fiancé, Princess."

I can't help the grin that spreads across my face as a wicked idea comes to my mind. I quickly open the shoebox to find a pair of black Gucci high heels. Placing them on the floor, I bend down slightly with my back to the door.

"Come in," I call out, knowing full well what the Prince will see first.

The minute the door opens, a gasp comes from his mouth. I look up, meeting his eyes in the mirror. He stands still, staring at me. His eyes bore into mine with something dark, something intense …

A crimson blush spreads over my body. His eyes darken as they rake over my body from head to toe.

"What can I help you with, Prince Benjamin?"

"I thought you would be ready by now," he whispers in his deep voice. I can practically see his jaw clenching and arms tightening as his muscles bulge against his black tux.

"There is still time, so if you have nothing important to say, you should probably wait outside." After putting on my heels, I pick up the jewelry and start placing the pieces in their respective spots.

When I look up in the mirror, he still hasn't left; instead, he is leaning back against the wall with his legs crossed and his hands resting in his pant pockets.

"Yes?" I ask.

"I said nothing."

"So why are you still here?" I ask while crossing my arms.

"I'd rather enjoy this stunning view than wait downstairs."

"Whatever suits you," I murmur with an eye roll and go to grab my gown. I put on the gown, acting as if he really isn't in the room, but I can feel the heat of his gaze upon me the entire time.

This was supposed to be a game of torture for him, but it seems like I'm the one who got played. Butterflies start churning in my belly as I zip up my dress. Returning back to the dressing table, I pick up the bracelet he got for me, cuffing it around my wrist.

Suddenly, I hear him striding toward me, his polished shoes tapping against the wooden floor. He grabs my wrist, but instead of desire, there is something else in his eyes. Confusion. Anger. Suspicion.

"Who gave this to you?" he asks.

"You did. I saw it on the table when I got to my room after lunch." I frown in confusion.

"I didn't give it to you. I just got the shoes, dress, earrings, and necklace. Did you bring it from home?"

I shake my head. Suddenly, the realization hits me. I think about a random stranger coming to my room and dropping this. Has he been here before? Is he among the guards? The servants?

My breathing accelerates as panic overtakes me. Calloused hands cup my face, making me look up to my prince. He is gazing at me with determination and confidence.

"Emma, listen to me. I promised to protect you, and I will. I won't let anything happen to you," he says.

"Why do you care so much about me? You barely know me."

He offers a gentle smile. "Would you believe it if I said it was because I love you?"

I gasp. *He loves me? When? How? Why?*

As if the questions were reflecting on my face, he answers them all. "I know you must be having a lot of queries. The truth is, I fell in love with you when I first saw your picture, but I kept myself at a distance, thinking you were like the other spoiled princesses. I was wrong. Every other princess spends her money on charities just for show and spends the rest on designer shit. Not you."

He skims his index finger along my cheeks. "You have spent millions from your trust fund on the poor, sick, homeless, orphaned, and even senior citizens. You never show off by calling the media or press about your charitable activities. You help them because they truly need it, not because the world needs to see it. That's what I truly admire about you. You are a true princess."

"I ... I never knew ... I don't know what to say," I whisper.

He shakes his head. "You don't have to say the words back. The feeling may not be mutual, but I will make you fall in love with me. I want my queen by my side 'til death do us part."

My eyes cast down. *Maybe ... I am already in love.* I almost say the words aloud, but he takes my hand and gives me my mask for the masquerade.

"Now let's go. Don't worry. I won't let anything happen to you," he promises, planting a soft kiss on my forehead.

CHAPTER 6

I see a line of expensive cars and limos heading up the driveway of the mansion. In the early evening light, the golden paper lanterns brighten the entryway as we get closer. I glance at Benjamin, who is now tying his mask, looking dark and mysterious in his raven-black Colombina mask.

He grins while looking back at me. "The mask makes your eyes look so beautiful. Absolutely elegant," he whispers, holding my hand in his.

I'm wearing the same mask, but mine is studded with diamonds at the corners. Excitement blooms inside me as the car halts, and we get out to join the party.

"Prince Benjamin! A picture, please," a few photographers nearly shout, already clicking photos of us.

The flashlights almost blind my eyes. *God, I hate the media.* Benjamin excuses us politely, avoiding the chaos to enter a new, different one.

The mansion is full. Politicians, princes, princesses, kings, queens, and reporters are all present. Everyone's attire matches with the dress code. *Wow. The place is packed.*

After taking two champagne glasses from a passing waiter, Benjamin hands me one. I definitely need it. I feel his eyes on me as I finish the glass in two gulps.

"What?" I ask.

He shakes his head. "Nothing. Let's go mingle."

For the next hour, we greet the other guests and watch more people file in. My cheeks hurt from the fake smile I have had plastered on my face since we got here. Benjamin, on the other hand, looks like he is at ease talking with so many people. Every now and then, I feel his dark eyes lingering on me, making my skin burn. Every time I meet his gaze, I'm reminded of our passionate kiss. I can still feel his lips on mine.

We stand in the corner of the room while talking with the king and queen of Alberta. The last time I saw them was on my seventeenth birthday, and they haven't changed much—neither has their obsession with the topic of opera. I never understood what it is with the royals and their fascination with opera. I never understand a single word of it.

"The one in Italy was so beautifully sung, I was mesmerized," the queen said, taking a little sip from her glass of red wine.

"The opera houses there are absolutely stunning," Benjamin noted, his hands resting on my back the whole time.

The king is talking about some political affair when I feel Benjamin's hand skating down, reaching for my ass. My breath hitches for a second, and I give him a look as if he has lost his mind.

His expression gives nothing away as if he is having a normal conversation like everyone else here. He gives my ass a tight squeeze, nearly making me jump. I manage to control my body, but how the hell do I control the arousal I feel spiking up?

He smirks at me as his hand lowers. He reaches between my ass, and I feel his fingers rubbing against my already wet lips through my dress.

Holy shit. I gulp, trying so hard to control my breathing while his fingers torture me. He traces my pussy lips as he resumes talking with the king.

"Dear, are you alright?" the queen asks me.

I nod frantically. "Yeah ... perfect." I barely manage to answer, biting on my tongue. I can feel my legs shaking already. I swear, if he continues this any further, I'm surely going to come. I think I'll be able to hold it off it he stops.

As if the bastard could read my mind, he removes his fingers. I groan from deep inside as I clench my jaw, feeling frustrated. *Fucking bastard! Ugh!*

When another guest comes to interact with the king and queen, I turn to face Benjamin. What he does next makes all the air leave my lungs as I watch him, spellbound.

He slips his fingers into his mouth and licks them clean while his eyes close in ecstasy. "*Mm* ... so good. Way better than the champagne," he whispers before leaning forward and planting a kiss below my ear.

"I wonder how it would taste mixed with champagne. Maybe we can find out later … what do you say?" he asks, presenting that devilish smirk.

What do I say? I have no fucking clue because my mind is completely blank after witnessing such an intense scenario. "I-I'll be r-right back," I stammer, whirling around and leaving him to go to the restroom. I need a break.

Walking out of the ballroom, I take the hallway that leads upstairs. Just as I reach the end of the hallway, a hand grabs my elbow and drags me inside a room. I hear the door's lock clicking, and immediate panic overwhelms me. Fear lurches through me.

What the …? Before I can scream for help, the same hand curls around my mouth, hampering my attempt to save myself. But when the man comes out of the shadows, relief courses through me.

"It's okay. I'm here to save you," the man speaks in his deep voice as he removes his hand from my mouth. "Just don't make a scene."

I frown in confusion. "Save me? The guards are here, and so is Benjamin … save me from what, Father?" I look around and see that we are in a dimly-lit office.

"I had to come and save you. After someone left that bracelet in your room, I knew Benjamin wouldn't be able to protect you. I'll call my guards and tell them to get you out of here safely," he mumbles while pacing the room, his shaky hands typing something on a phone screen.

"No, Father. He promised me that he would protect me—"

"What rubbish. Don't trust him. We will be out of here soon."

I can easily sense the tension in my father's voice. I walk up to him, placing my hand on his shoulder for reassurance. "Father, believe me. He can protect me."

"Emma, don't argue with me and do as you are told." He turns around, focusing back on the text message.

My heart starts pounding against my chest. I don't want to leave Benjamin so soon. *God, I knew telling Father about the whole bracelet incident was a bad idea ... wait. How does he know?*

"Father, who told you about someone coming to my room and placing the bracelet there?" I ask.

"Benjamin told me before entering the party," he answers, facing me.

It can't be. "That's not possible. Benjamin was with me the whole time, and he didn't make any calls. So I'll ask you again. How did you know?"

Just then, the office door opens with a *bang*. I watch as Benjamin strides in with a gun in his hand and his bodyguards right behind him.

"Emma, get away from your father!" he growls, raising his hand to point the gun at my dad.

When I turn around, I see my dad in the same posture, gun in hand.

"Emma, don't listen to him. Come to me. I'll keep you safe—"

"He is the one, Emma. There is no threat from a strange person. He set it all up," Benjamin explains, taking a step forward. "After your mother died, her trust fund was moved into your name. He needs the money because he is going bankrupt. He was even planning to kill you to get all the money!"

Agony hits me hard as I realize that my own father wants to kill me.

"Emma, he is lying. He is the one who set it up. You are engaged. He plans to get your trust fund by marrying and killing you. That's why I came here to save you. Listen to your father, Emma," Father says, sounding desperate.

I look back and forth between the two men on both sides. One is telling the truth, and the other is lying. Do I go to the man who raised me after my mother died, or to the man who I've known for only a few days, but I trust with all my heart?

When I look at Benjamin, I see it in his eyes … the truth. I move to walk toward him, but my father instantly grabs my neck, pulling me to him. He raises the gun against my skull, keeping me close to his chest.

"Don't make a fucking move, or I'll shoot her! Drop your gun, Benjamin, and tell your guards to drop theirs too!" Father yells, pressing the gun harder against my skin.

No. No. No. This can't be happening. Tears start streaming down my cheeks as I feel the betrayal strike my heart. The fact that my own father betrayed me for money makes my heart clench. "Father, please—"

"Shut up! God knows why your mother left you with the money! *I* needed it, not you! But I will still get it, and this time, it will be from your fiancé."

My eyes widen with fear as I hear the safety lock clicking off my father's gun.

"I said, drop your guns!" he yells, nearly bursting my eardrums.

With wide eyes, I watch Benjamin look helpless and unsure. With no other choice, he starts to lower his gun.

No. I won't let this happen. Taking the opportunity, I kick my father's shin, hearing him growl in pain. I don't waste a second as I rush to Benjamin, who immediately draws his gun and fires at my father. At the same time, another shot rings out, and Benjamin's body instantly falls to the ground with a thud.

No! Taking off my mask and his, I kneel down in front of him. Blood starts to coat his white shirt as it runs down to the wood floor. Tears instantly burst from my eyes and course down my cheeks.

"No! Benjamin! Stay with me! Someone call an ambulance!"

Some of the guards are busy handling my father, while three others help me with Benjamin, whose eyes are becoming drowsy as his body turns limp.

"Benjamin, please! Don't leave me. I love you," I whisper to his ear, earning a mere grin.

"Told you I will always protect you …" he says, his voice trailing off as his eyes close.

CHAPTER 7

It's been two weeks since the night of the gala. Two things happened that night. First, my father was arrested and is now serving fifteen years in prison for attempted murder. Second, Benjamin was shot and was immediately taken to the hospital for surgery. I still remember how my heart pounded against my chest as I feared for his life. After six hours, the doctor told us his condition was stabilized and that he needed bed rest. I can't describe how relieved I was. Tears of joy coated my eyes.

I almost lost him once, and I never want to let it happen again. I have been taking care of him since the minute we got back home. The more time we spend together, the more it feels as if I am falling in love with him all over again. Watching him get back on his feet makes me feel so peaceful. It feels like there are no problems in our lives anymore, and we can finally move on.

I knock on his door, wearing a black shirt with matching jeans. Beneath it, I'm wearing a corset, black lace underwear, and stockings. After dinner, he told me to come straight to his room wearing the clothes set out for me on my bed. For the past few days, he would kiss me every time he got the chance, and touch me like a sneaky bastard, arousing me with his touch only.

He opens the door to me, already dressed in a black shirt and pants with his sleeves rolled, showing off his stony muscles. He has a glass of scotch in his hand, and I can see the bulge against his pants. Knowing what is going to happen, a thrill runs through me. Am I ready for it?

"May I come in?" I whisper.

"All obedient now, are we?" His voice is deeper than usual.

I flush, casting my eyes downward.

"I actually like you feisty; it's one of the things I love about you, among other things, Princess." He winks at me before moving aside to let me enter. He takes my hand and lifts it to his mouth, kissing it softly.

"Today, I'm going to show you my other side that I don't reveal often. If you feel uncomfortable at any time, let me know, and it all will stop. You have my word, Emma."

I nod with a gentle smile. "I trust you."

With a soft smile, he gives me a swift kiss on the lips before leading me inside his room. I glance around and note the changes. A flogger, handcuffs, and a riding crop rest on the bed. There are even two chains hanging from the ceiling. I swallow the lump in my throat and try to ignore the nerves dancing in my stomach.

He positions me with the chains right above me before he retrieves the handcuffs. "Strip," he commands.

I take my shirt off, followed by my jeans, and stand in front of him, wearing only the lingerie. He smiles darkly as he takes my hands, cuffs them, and hooks the ends to the chain, raising both my hands up. After securing my bounds, he steps back, puts his hands inside his pockets, and takes in my sight. His hungry eyes drop to my bare belly as he moves forward and draws lazy circles with the back of his hand. My breath hitches from just the single touch. He walks around me like a hunter circling his prey. Benjamin gets the crop from his bed, slapping the end against his palm lightly.

My eyes widen for a moment. *Oh, my God.* "You are going to start with *that* already? No foreplay?" I ask. *Well, he did ask for my feisty side …*

He smirks. "You are already wet; I can smell it from here. So why waste time with foreplay? I didn't say you could talk—"

"I'm also a part of this scenario, so I can—" I don't get to finish my words before the crop slaps against my breast, making me squeal.

"Be quiet; otherwise, you will be punished, Princess," he warns.

I gulp. The crop traces my breasts before it slips down my belly and reaches the apex of my thighs. He waits for a few seconds before slapping my skin. I gasp as he traces my wet lips with the crop and lands a slap there as well. I can't help but moan aloud as I pull on the restraints. *Holy fuck.*

While Benjamin watches my reaction, amusement floats in his eyes. He rains continuous slaps down on my pussy while I buck and shiver, almost screaming.

"Do you want to come?" he asks.

"Yes! Please!" I can feel my muscles dancing on the edge, and I know I'm about to come.

"Then beg for it, Princess," he orders.

My eyes are tightly closed as I try to compose myself. "Please … *please*, Benjamin," I beg.

Slap. "Please what?"

"Please make me come. I need it."

"With my fingers or the crop? This time, you choose, and choose wisely as I will make you come twice in a row."

My insides tighten upon hearing his promise. "The crop," I answer instantly. God knows if he tortures me with his fingers, I'll die right on this spot.

He sneers. "So eager, but as you wish."

With that, he slaps my wet pussy with the crop mercilessly. My entire body is on fire, and I'm about to combust any minute now. *More. I need more.* I've never felt this alive. I can't get away from him, even if I wanted to, which I don't. Oh, God, I don't.

The orgasm explodes through me with an intensity I never imagined. I see white for a second as my knees buckle. By the time I open my eyes, he has already undressed and is standing there completely naked and hard. Muscles ripple in his abdomen, and he has a *V* of perfect definition that drops to his groin. His cock is fully erected against his stomach, and precum spreads all over his length as he strokes himself a few times.

"I thought I would torture you further, but now I can't help myself. I need to get a taste," he growls.

Standing in front of me, he cups my face and kisses me deeply, his tongue tangling with mine. I moan in appreciation. I am tracing his bottom lip with my tongue when, suddenly, I hear a rip and feel exposed all of a sudden. Looking down, I find my panties now torn in half on the floor.

Without wasting another second, he kneels down. "I want to suck you so badly. I want to taste every inch of you."

Fucking God.

He places tender kisses on the inside of my thigh, enticing a quiver from my body. "Stay still. Move an inch and see what happens." His eyes hold mine as his tongue traces my wet lips.

I try not to buck against him, I really do. He grabs my thighs and pulls them open as he begins sucking on my sex. His eyes are filled with lust and something … dark.

I pull on the chains, trying to control my reactions. The pleasure mounts as he sucks harder and faster. My body shivers as an intense arousal that I've never felt before builds with every passing second. I'm so lost in his touch that I can't think of anything but his tongue on my pussy.

"Such a good girl. Come for me now."

As if his words work like a button, I come instantly with a scream. My entire body quivers and shakes as I feel his strong arms around my waist while he kisses me.

"So good, Princess. You did so well," he whispers in my ear while unclasping the cuffs.

My arms immediately give out and wrap around his neck. He picks me up and takes me to his bed.

"I'm not finished with you, Emma. On your hands and knees," he commands.

Christ … I roll over and do as I am told.

He grabs my ass harshly before giving my right cheek a hard spank. I squeal and almost move forward, but he holds me in place. He kisses the small of my back as he slides a finger into my pussy.

"Ah …" I scrunch my eyes shut.

"Still so wet. So fucking hot."

His lips stay on my back as his fingers slowly work me, pulling me against him until I sit in his lap. I close my eyes as pleasure shoots through me.

"You like that, Princess?"

"God, yes!"

He keeps pushing his fingers in and out, never stopping. Suddenly, I feel his cock as he lines himself up and pushes forward. I scream as a searing pain burns through me.

"Oh!" I cry out.

He turns my face toward him, kissing me deeply as he masks my screams, turning them into moans of pleasure. "It's okay, Princess. Just breathe. I have you."

His hand goes to my clit, and he circles his fingers with just the right pressure to make me feel pleasure instead of pain. My eyes roll back in my head, and he starts moving … in and out. In and out.

"Ah, God," I whimper.

"That's it." He pulls out and pushes back in as slowly as he can.

I push back against him and hear him growl, "Baby, let's take this slow; otherwise, I won't be able to control myself."

"Don't hold back. I want you … *all* of you." I push back again, and he hisses.

He slides in and out a few times and then gradually speeds up. I begin to bounce back into him, relieved that the pain has stopped and that it is now only pleasure building up. He grabs my hipbones and begins to thrust inside me as I hold my breath. The sound of our skin slapping and harsh breathing is all I hear. I turn my head to face him and see his lustful eyes fixed on mine. Both of us are wet with perspiration, and he's taking my body however he wants it. He increases the pressure on my clit as I'm on the verge of reaching my orgasm.

"Fuck, Emma. Come with me," he hisses.

I scream as a tornado of an orgasm rips through me, tearing me apart. Benjamin tips his head back, groaning his appreciation as he comes deep inside me. For a while, he moves slowly, in and out, on repeat. Eventually, he kisses my back and neck as he comes to lie over me, his cock still inside me.

"I love you, Benjamin. I love every version of you," I whisper.

"I love you too, my queen."

"Queen? I thought I was your princess," I say with a giggle.

"You have been the queen of my heart since day one, Emma," he whispers, kissing the back of my ear.

"Even when I'm royally feisty?" I tease him.

He chuckles. "Especially when you are royally feisty."

Springtime Kisses

January Wren

Sacha leaned against the doorway, his dark gaze washing over his princess. He knew that he would find her in their living room, the same as he once had found her in her quarters, where she stayed apart from her husband. She had taken to keeping to herself, so unlike how she had been as a little girl. She had reveled in the company of others, and taken to silent rooms only when she slept, though the songbirds she adored soon woke her with their song.

Now, there were times when Louise withdrew from him and kept her own company, her brow furrowing, and her teeth sinking into her bottom lip while he watched her from afar. What did she wonder? What did she dream of? Sacha scoffed at himself, knowing that she was a girl no longer. She hadn't been since her marriage, nor was he a boy any longer.

Louise hummed softly to herself as she knelt over May, a green-eyed and bushy-tailed tabby that he had given her. She held a stick in one hand, a leather fish dangling from the end of it. May was intent on catching the fish.

"Such a silly kitty," Louise said with a laugh as the cat caught the fish's head and brought it to her mouth.

May gummed on it, her eyes narrowing as she tasted the catnip.

"You're a fierce warrior, aren't you?"

Sacha's lip curled upward. If any of the mortals who lived nearby knew that the raggedy-looking cat that roamed the woods was actually a chimera, a fantastic, mythical creature, they would have gone running to the nearest church. May was content to hunt mice and grasshoppers now, but in the months to come, she would develop a taste for bloody steaks and imps that hid beneath their beds. There were more than Fae that hid amidst mortals, as he and Louise had learned. Thankfully, no matter how fierce May was, the slim collar on her neck kept her illusioned to the mortal eye.

"Your Grace," Sacha murmured.

Louise glanced over her shoulder at him, her grey eyes holding his. "You called me by my name, once," she replied, her voice light. "Won't you again?"

As children, they had entangled freely together. He was an illegitimate child of Winter, while she was an acknowledged daughter of Spring. Sacha was twelve when his uncle brought him to the Spring Court, one that abounded with delirious life and pleasure. It was a far cry from the Winter Court that prided itself on ceremony and rank.

"You'll have a chance here, boy," his uncle had told him after finding him employment in the royal menagerie. He knew his nephew had a talent for working with animals ever since the boy had calmed his warhorse with his voice alone. "More than you ever had as a bastard in your father's court."

Sacha knew that his father's nature was widely mocked. Some courtiers remarked that his father acted as if the Fae were dwindling, and he thought to raise their numbers through his own generosity alone.

The Winter Court held little opportunity for the king's illegitimate children and their mothers. Sacha knew little of his mother, despite how he wondered; was she a Fae? Was she a human whom the king had found in a Fae circle? Sacha never asked his nursemaid, nor his uncle after he came to the Spring Court.

It matters not, he told himself, and his uncle seemed to think the same. His uncle never spoke of whether he had known his mother, or if he knew the circumstances of his birth. Sacha was a tool for his ambitions, as his uncle was acting as a steward for the king, and had many indebted to him. His nephew was the same as the others, which was a truth that they both knew. It became truer still as Sacha found himself in the company of an unwanted princess.

Before Sacha came to court, he heard little of Princess Louise, the acknowledged but unwanted daughter of Prince Francois. As the crowned heir, Francois impatiently waited for when his father would fall.

It was said that Prince Francois's ambitions had been tempered when he first married his wife, a distant relation from the Fall Court. It was said that Princess Anne had been the love of his youth, as they enchanted the court with fetes and laughter.

Yet the prince's fascination with her faded with every daughter she bore, for only males could inherit in the Spring Court, and Francois wanted an heir of his own before he assumed the throne. "An heir and a spare," every royal female knew, was their husband's due.

The prince's heart turned sullen when the queen bore a fourth daughter, and he had refused to come to her bedside when she burned with fever. It was said that the princess had whispered their newborn's name, "Reina Louise," as if naming the girl as queen would forgive her horrid, wrong anatomy.

It hadn't, as the weary Princess Anne passed and was buried without fanfare, and the last daughter was left to her nanny and governess. Her first name, Reina, was quickly dropped, and she was only referred to by her middle name, Louise. Even the princess, Sacha later knew, shook her head at her first name. Her siblings, old enough to follow the example of their father and his court, had little interest in her, and Louise was left as *persona non grata.* It only deepened as Prince Francois remarried and sired a son only ten months after their binding.

Louise was left to exist on the fringes of the court, where distant relatives, forgotten dowagers, and minor aristocrats gathered. She was never allowed the company of her siblings, nor did she know what it was like to sit on her father's knee while he sang her praises to the assembled court.

Is she the same as I am? Sacha wondered. Did Louise know what it was like to feel the overwhelming heat of the kitchens? Did she learn every hidden stairway and hallway that only the servants used? Did Louise know what it was like to be alone? She did, Sacha later learned, when they whispered to each other late into the night.

Louise spent most of her life amidst the servants and was kept away from her family. The servants grew used to having her underfoot; the servants that remembered her mother and her sweet manner treated Louise with affection, while others ignored her, for fear of her father.

It only worsened as she aged and looked like a replica of her mother, with her gray eyes, sweet and timid smile, and dark curls that she wore in thick braids down her back. Her skin was often kissed by the sun as she spent hours outside, in sharp contrast to other females at court. She laughed easily and happily as if she was unrestrained by the world and its expectations. If she had been allowed to, she would have drawn every courtier and servant to her side, but fear of her father kept them away.

Nothing was as esteemed as loyalty to the royal family, every servant and courtier knew. Sacha knew it too. His uncle had ingratiated himself into the deepest folds at court and kept his fingers on the very pulse of it. Being without children, his uncle wanted to forge Sacha into his most flavorful tool, one that could take after him.

"Let the court find you as kind and humble as a maid," his uncle soon instructed after Sacha proved himself well at court, "until they forget you exist at all."

Sacha found that his uncle's instructions were true, as he proved himself a hard worker at the menagerie, and that his quiet nature invited others to talk to him. They soon loosened their tongues and relied on him for his discretion, many pressing notes into his hand and pleading for him to deliver the notes and accompanying gifts to a lover, or two.

It was then, as Sacha had slunk through the hallways with a lover's ring in his pocket, that he came across a charming princess. He had caught the kitten that she was chasing, and he adjusted the ribbon tied loosely around its neck before setting it back in her arms. She had thanked him with a clumsy curtsy, her flower crown slipping from her head, and he found himself distracted, wanting to linger beside her, something that his uncle had never warned him about.

Sacha strode across the room and knelt at her side. The rug beneath them was plush and faux fur, a far cry from the stone floors of the Spring Palace.

"You know that I have little right to your name, Your Grace," he said lowly.

He would tuck her against his side if he could, wrapping his arm around her shoulder as if he had a right to … as if he were her lover, in truth.

It had taken little for them to take to one another as children after their meeting in the hall. Sacha found that Louise moved her songbirds from her room to the menagerie instead, and she came every day to see them.

"And you," Louise added when Sacha remarked on her daily visits. "I want to see you too, Sacha, though you don't sing as sweetly as they do," she teased, ducking her head.

He'd chuckled at that, the first time that he had laughed since coming to court.

Despite the six years between them, Sacha soon found himself calling her his friend. They met inside and out the royal menagerie, two lonely children in want of company. They read together and played in the golden fields, and Louise would braid flowers in his dark curls.

He had been the first to teach her how to ride a horse, instructing her on how to mount her dappled pony and hold the reins firmly in her hands. The handful of times that she had fallen, her lower lip had quivered, and her cheeks had flushed until he'd offered his hand for her to stand once more. Sacha found that he took an inordinate amount of pleasure in teaching her. She looked to him for guidance and approval, as if he were important to her. He wanted to keep her safe from the world as if she was a field mouse that he could tuck into his pocket and keep watch over.

The few courtiers who noticed had sneered and called her their *chienne* as if she were a hound in heat. French was the favored language of the Spring Court, as the Fae devoured tales of mortal royalty and their own practices. Most held a fascination for the human world, trapping humans within their Fae circles in order to glean their thoughts and their words. He was grateful that she had never asked what they meant; instead, she chattered to him about the rats that she fed in the kitchens and the spider that spun elegant webs in her quarters.

Everything had changed when Louise was in her fourteenth year and showed the same skill that her mother's family was noted for. She had life flowing through her veins, as she brought wilted flowers into healthy bloom, and her tears brought a stillborn foal to rise and canter through the field. It was skillful magic that had escaped Louise's mother, as she had never been able to prevent the death of her children and her repeated loss of pregnancy.

Sacha saw the magic that resided inside her, having been at her side when the foal came to life, and was forced to bear the news to his father. He knew that if he hadn't, his uncle would have wanted him to burn, and he would have lost his place at court. Fae couldn't survive on their own, exiled to the seasonless lands that lie beyond the four kingdoms. Sacha had no secrets of his own, save for the smiles that Louise gave him and the moments they laughed together. Beyond that, Sacha had nothing he could hide in his heart or the cavern of his ribs.

Their paths were set then, as Louise became a focus of the court, and her father became king. She was gifted new apartments, a set that overlooked the court gardens, and her sisters held teas that she was invited to. Sacha was trusted by his uncle far more than before, as the news he'd passed had proven true. Louise had life at her fingertips, a fanciful talent that kept death away.

It was Louise who knew him best still, the childhood friend who had become ever more to him. She held little judgment against him for revealing her gifts to his uncle, both of them knowing that the court was ever watchful and knowing. Little secrets were kept still, but none from her father now that he was king.

It was her name that Sacha had on his lips, in the privacy of his rooms, when he imagined what it would be like to chastely kiss her and pledge himself to her. It was a fanciful dream, the kind that he had never allowed himself before.

It was fruitless, as Louise soon attracted the attention of a Winter lord. He came from across the snow-covered ocean, hearing of the little princess's talent for making life flourish beneath her fingertips. He needed her talent, as life was faltering in the northernmost lands.

Their marriage came to pass when she turned seventeen, and she boarded a ship to cross the distance between them. Sacha was allowed to accompany her, as her father had allowed her only a small retinue, with Sacha's uncle arranging who went.

"Your ties will help the princess," his uncle had told him, as if Sacha had been raised amidst the Winter Court and not the Spring. "She will have to learn their ways and become one of the Winter without forgoing her Spring loyalties."

During the months it took to cross the ocean, Louise turned eighteen. She had asked only for a kiss from Sacha, batting her eyelashes at him until he had chuckled with drunken laughter. He had allowed her to taste the whiskey that he preferred to drink for the first time, and had drunk at her side.

"Please?" Louise had asked him, and he'd been a fool to give in to her.

Her lips had been tender and sweet as he pressed his lips against hers. His tongue had skimmed against the seam of her lips, and she had parted hers for him, allowing him in. It had been for several blissful moments that they had kissed, and she had tangled her hands in his hair before he had forced himself away from her.

"Sacha," she had whispered, her breath warm against his face.

"Your Grace," he'd replied, closing his eyes as she flinched. He had always used her first name when they were alone, a familiarity existing between them as if they were more than friends … as if they were equals. It was something that they would never be, especially upon her engagement and subsequent marriage. They could never be if Sacha was to keep her safe. "I live to serve you, Your Grace."

His service had taken them to where they were now, two of the Fae, hiding away amidst humans. "I won't go back, you know," Louise said, her tone earnest. "I can't, Sacha, not after …" She swallowed tautly.

They both knew what hid beneath her nightgowns, her skin marked with more than it ever should have been.

"I know," Sacha hesitated her name on his lips like honeyed sin. *Louise*. "I know."

The Winter Court had changed little since he was a child. It clung to ceremony still, and its hierarchy was even more rigid than it had been in the past. His apartments were near Louise only because of the position he was given, Sacha knew. He was her personal guard, shadowing her as if he were her familiar. He was, truth be told, with how he followed her so.

Louise's husband was two decades older than she was, and had been married before; his first wife was as barren as the frigid world outside. Their vows were filled with odes to fertility, and Sacha had drunk himself silly after what had occurred on their wedding night.

Louise had run through the halls, her slippered feet slapping against the marble until she found his door. He was used to little sleep and had been sitting before the fire with a tumbler of whiskey in his hand. When he heard her frantic knock, he threw it into the roaring flames before opening the bedroom door to her.

"Your Grace," Sacha had murmured. He then found himself holding her as she threw herself into his arms.

It was the same as when she had been a child, and he had taught her how to ride. Her gentle mare had been startled by a snake in the grass and had thrown her to the ground. He had brushed the dirt from her shoulders and helped her up then, crooning reassuring words to her as her lower lip wobbled. She hadn't allowed herself to cry, rapidly blinking until she asked for him to help her mount again. Only this time, her tears fell freely.

He had pulled her into his room and closed the door behind her. She had been desperate for comfort as she clung to him and nuzzled her cheek against his chest. She whispered that her husband had done things to her, things that made Sacha realize her new husband had taken her without care.

He drew her to his bed, where he allowed her to slip beneath the covers before he retreated to the privy that adjoined his quarters. There, he had stripped fabric from his robe before he wetted it with water and returned to her.

"I'm here, Your Grace."

"Sacha, please," she'd whispered, her gray eyes meeting his. "Call me by name."

He'd lowered to sit beside her and tenderly ran the damp fabric over her flushed cheeks. "You know that I cannot," he'd told her, his voice softer than even hers was.

She pushed the covers down past her waist as silence reigned between them. He'd inhaled as he saw the opaque fluid on her thighs, and moved to wipe it away. She hissed at the feeling, and Sacha was unsurprised as he saw crimson mingled with her husband's seed.

"Will it always be this way?" she had asked.

He didn't ask whether she referred to her marriage bed or the changed relationship between them. "It shouldn't be," Sacha replied, his voice low.

He slowly ran the cloth over her skin, watching as her skin became clean again. Yet he knew that it wasn't that easy, as the crisscrossed scars on his own body proclaimed. His life at the Winter Court hadn't always been easy, nor was it fair before his uncle had claimed him. Yet he'd hoped, for Louise's sake, that she found what he never had at the Winter Court—acceptance, if not love from the courtiers and her husband. Sacha was cruel to hope that things would improve.

As the months passed and Louise remained without a child, her husband became as displeased as her father had. "How is it," her husband often said, "that Louise may bring a stillborn foal to life, yet she brings nothing forth from her cunt?"

Her room became without decoration as her husband withdrew from her, as did the ladies who attended to her. There was little support that came from the Spring Court; Louise was as unimportant to her family as she had been before her gifts were discovered. Her place at the Winter Court would become secure only when she proved herself fertile.

Only Sacha remained, unflinchingly, by her side. He ceased writing letters to his uncle and ignored the frequent notes that his relative sent in turn. He knew how his uncle loathed his silence, yet he wouldn't betray Louise. Not again, no, never again.

It was near Louise and her lord's anniversary when things changed between them. Louise sat on a chaise near the window, with her knees drawn against her chest and her arms wrapped around them. Sacha's gaze was drawn to the bruise marring her cheek, and the tears that dripped down from her chin.

"Your Grace—"

"He was angry," Louise whispered, a woman in place of the girl that she had been, "so very angry, Sacha."

He came to kneel before her, not wanting to intimidate her with his height, as he did with some. Sacha knew that he was considered a distinguished figure, with his generous nose, dark curls that rested at his nape, and sapphire-colored eyes, while others whispered that he was a hideous beast. He had a cold manner about him, one that drove others away. Perhaps his mother had felt the same.

"He should treat you kindly," Sacha murmured. *As kindly as I would.* The words went unsaid as his nails sunk into the tender flesh of his palm. He had drawn rivets of blood before, the wooden floors having permanent stains from his actions.

Louise unwound her limbs, moving to sit before him. He was unmoving and silent as she moved, and her hands came to cradle his face.

"I know," Louise whispered, the words solely between them, unable to be heard if anyone was listening outside her door. "Yet I've failed him, haven't I?"

He made a noise of appreciation as her hands cradled his face, and her thumb stroked his bottom lip.

"It's been two years," Louise said, and Sacha knew that she was referring to the length of her marriage. "My lord, he … he expects more from me."

Sacha kept himself still as he held her soft inhale.

"Do you think I am like her?" Louise asked, her lips trembling as she swallowed. "Princess Anne? My mother?"

Sacha was silent a moment, knowing what she was truly asking him. "He will not set you aside, Your Grace," he said slowly. "Your talents would flourish if you were allowed sunlight and life around you."

Louise's husband preferred for her to keep to her small and cloistered rooms, which overlooked an abandoned courtyard where nothing would keep except the sticks and stones that crows dropped there. It was a snow-covered world outside the Winter Court's doors, one where frigid temperatures abounded, and ice clung everywhere it could.

It was a struggle for any flower and fauna to survive, and Louise could bring little to life when she had nothing that bloomed inside her. Sacha had watched as she withdrew to her own quarters, where she read countless books or played with the elegant hound that he had procured for her.

Outside of his visits to his mistress, the lord did little outside, despite having elaborate plans designed for a garden that would withstand the bitter temperatures. It had proven impossible; no matter how many saplings and seeds they tried, nothing would take, only knowing how to die.

It was hardly a wonder why Louise was withering inside. There was no allowance for life in the North, where everything was clinging to survive. "Perhaps a visit to the eastern provinces would soothe you," Sacha continued, knowing the temperatures were less extreme there. "The lord could be persuaded—"

"She is with child again," Louise whispered. "Marie."

It was well known throughout the Winter Court that Louise's husband had a mistress. A low born noble, Marie had attracted the lord's interest on her first visit to court and had born him several children. Louise's husband refused to put her aside, declaring that he was well pleased with her.

"Is she?"

Louise nodded. "A decade older than I am, yet life thrives inside her."

"It would thrive inside you if given a chance," Sacha insisted, his fist clenching.

There was little malice to her voice; instead, there was a thread of sorrow that made Sacha's heartache. He had watched her with children before. She would gather a lady-in-waiting's newborn to her chest and gently soothe his cries while his mother embroidered beside her. There was an innate kindness inside her that Sacha adored, a feeling that he buried deep inside him and wouldn't allow free, even in his dreams. If only that was the truth.

"Do you remember the first time I knelt at your feet?" Sacha murmured.

It was the second time that she had cried before him after her marriage. She hadn't grown to accept her husband's touch and had kept to her rooms after he left for the court. Sacha had found her on the same velvet chaise, with a book in hand and tears streaming down her cheeks. He saw the hickeys that covered her neck and crept past the neckline of her dress.

"You are my princess," he'd told her the last time he had knelt at her feet, and he showed her how gentle he could be. "Your husband's family, the court, and the world outside would adore you if they knew you in truth."

"Do you truly believe so?" she'd asked, as if she were a young girl looking to him again. It was a look that he knew well, having known her then. "I have no influence here, Sacha. You ... you owe nothing to me. I," she paused, her teeth sinking into her lower lip, "I have nothing that matters but your friendship."

She wanted everything from him ... his approval, his acceptance, and his familiar company.

"You are my life," he told her, the words heavy on his tongue. "Louise."

Sacha knew that he would burn for the thoughts he later had of her, the sweet princess who made him flower crowns and called on him by name. She was a woman ever above him, one who had bloomed and withered before him. He wanted her to live again, the same as she had when she was a child, with her hand tucked in his.

"This is madness," she'd whispered, as he dusted kisses across her soft skin. It was a sin that he would willingly burn for. She shivered beneath his attention. His teeth lightly scraped her skin before he turned to kisses once more. Had anyone ever adored her?

He knew the answer as he trailed down her stomach, his hands bunching her cotton gown upward. He kissed the flat of her stomach and heard her quiet whimper as he drew near her hip bone. He came across a small thatch of curls as he drew lower still, and he nuzzled his nose against them. Everything about her was tangy and sweet, the same as the honey that he had once spooned into his mouth, as a wanting child.

"Of the sweetest kind," he'd replied before he had buried his head between her legs.

Her lacy underwear had been pushed aside as he delved between her folds with his tongue and showed her what it was like to be loved. She had keened beneath his touch, a woman undone, as she'd buried her hands in his hair.

"Oh! Please!" she'd whimpered when his mouth had found her little pearl, and he'd suckled on it, the same as if he was a kitten lapping from a bowl of the sweetest milk. She bucked her hips against him, unable to escape his greedy mouth and his insistent tongue. "I've never felt anything like this before."

He eagerly swallowed the slickness that poured into his mouth as she came, his hands holding her quivering thighs apart. He knew that, for as long as he lived, he would remember the moment between them, and the taste of her cunt on his tongue. He wanted to give her everything that her husband never had, and worship her body as if he had a right to. It was the most bittersweet dream, one that was always just out of reach.

She had drawn him up to her embrace afterward and panted in his ear as he slipped his fingers inside her. He had found the slickest part of her and fingered her there, reveling in the sweetness of it all. He had whispered encouragement into her ear while she ground against his hand and soon came undone again, her nerves on fire and lips parted. It was a sin that both of them would remember; he adored the musky taste of her and the scent of apple blossoms that clung to her skin, while she cherished the feel of his tongue, and how he had shown her what it was like to come undone.

Sacha watched as her cheeks tinged pink, knowing that she remembered their time together. She was sweetness incarnate, and he had no right to her, yet he wanted, *oh*, how he wanted her.

"I would give you anything that you asked for," he said, his voice grave. "Or anything that you need."

Their eyes met for a moment, his meaning well understood. If her husband's seed wouldn't take, perhaps another's would … one who shared the dark coloring of her husband, while retaining an unyielding sense of discretion and loyalty to the princess.

"I cannot ask this of you," Louise said, her eyes lowering from his. "I … " she hesitated, and her cheeks flushed darker than ever before. "I could never expect … *this* from you."

"Foolish girl," Sacha gently chided. "I am yours to serve, Your Grace."

It was this fealty that led them to where they were now. The cottage they stayed in was small and tucked away in a pretty village, its lawn outside trimmed and neat, with its side garden flourishing with life. It was known that every bird came to its backyard, and stray cats liked to roam the property before sleeping on its back porch.

Sacha had offered his princess a child, and she had asked him to free her instead.

"Run away with me," she whispered, as another month passed without her womb quickening.

Every courtier knew that her husband's patience was becoming undone, and he refused to visit her bed. His mistress was well pleased, the fascinated court following her lead, regardless of propriety.

"Please, Sacha."

Who was Sacha to dissuade her? He knew that the Fall Court would offer them little, as Louise's mother had only been a minor princess there. The Summer Court was where Louise's stepmother was from, and with her current marriage, it was doubtful they would be well received there.

"We can go nowhere amidst the Fae world, Your Grace," Sacha had thought aloud. "There will be little welcome for you amongst another court. Your family—"

They would offer her little protection if she returned to the Spring Court, and would most likely send her back to her raging husband. There was only one option left to them.

"The mortal realm then," Louise said. "We may find freedom there."

Every Fae knew of the realm outside their own, every court having a fascination for it. Human ways were not unknown to them, from their curious mating rites to their pretty stained glass window panes, an art that the Fae chose to emulate.

"If you're sure, Your Grace," Sacha said, ignoring the sharp look that she gave him.

He felt his heart thud harshly in his chest as he knew they would shed their wings to enter the mortal realm. Fae who walked amidst the mortals lost their Fae appearance; the pointed tips of their ears rounded, and wings burnt away, while their magic remained.

"We cannot return if you choose this way."

"If *we*," Louise corrected gently.

"If *we*," Sacha agreed, the words sweet on his tongue, for even then, he knew the choice that he would make.

He'd known it since she asked him to run away, and earlier still, when she'd come to him on her wedding night with tears streaming down her cheeks. He'd known that he would go wherever she wished and had made countless plans, ones that were nothing but ashes in the fireplace. In his heart, every plan was carved. His hands, his mouth, his cock, and his filthy, greedy heart all belonged to her.

There were things that he would teach her, if she asked, things that he would show her that she could hardly dream of. He would show her that there was love in every position, whether she was riding him and clinging to his shoulders, or wrapping her legs about his and thrashing beneath him. He would show her how he could arouse her with his fingers, stroking her clit and suckling at her breast until she whimpered his name.

He wanted to trace every freckle and follow every curve until he knew her body as well as she knew it herself. He wanted her to know his body in turn, and that she was the only one who would ever touch him as he allowed her in.

"I love you," he ached to say with every fiber of his being. "More than I will ever love another, Louise."

He wanted to know every cry and whimper that she had and every place that she liked to be touched. He wanted to know what made her heart flutter, and the sounds she made in the morning when she awoke to the sunlight kissing her skin as the birds sang to her. He wanted to see the world as it bloomed for her and to know that he had a place in her heart.

His mother had always said he was a greedy child, as he kept two nannies busy looking after him. He had always wanted whatever was in his sight … his father's treasured hound that accompanied him on hunts, the locket that hung from his mother's neck, and anything else that caught his attention. He remembered what he wanted and rarely forgot it, even after he'd had it and its owner took it back.

He never would court another, nor marry, as he served her alone. Her safety was ever at the forefront of his thoughts, and concern for her happiness tucked inside his heart. It was the same then, as it was now; Louise the only one that he looked to, regardless of the realm they belonged to. She was the only one that he had allowed to stumble her way in.

He had been lost to her as a boy, the same that he was as a man. If she had asked him to draw her husband closer to her, he would have, the same as he would have torn the lord's mistress away from him, if only to give his wife an earnest chance. Her feelings mattered more than his own, as he knew that his place was to serve her, no matter how she thought of him as her equal, or the mortal realm they now resided in.

He would stay at her side, without end, for it was always springtime in the mortal realm with Louise beside him. He always wanted her near, the same as his necessity to her remained. For he served her, Sacha reminded himself, in any way that she needed him. For there was a thought that coursed through him, one as small and as diligent as a worm hollowing out an apple. No Fae had entered the mortal realm and returned … but if there was one that could, it was Louise.

In his dreams, he saw her fashioning herself new wings and returning to the realm they both had known as their home. She assured him that she was happy in the mortal realm, and she had smiled more than he had ever seen her do since she was a child. Still, the thought haunted him, as Sacha would be without cause—without purpose—if she left without him.

Was he a coward? That thought had joined the other one too, a second worm, that crept inside him. Some days it felt as if there was a great distance between him and the one that he served, moments when Louise would lapse into silence, and he would hesitate to fill it. He wanted to hear her voice and know her touch, the same as he had been graced with once.

So, as Sacha watched his princess play with the chimera he'd bought for her before they'd left the Fae realm, he made another choice. He could be brave, he thought. He could. He reached for her free hand, tucking it into his calloused one.

"Sacha?" she asked, her eyes meeting his.

He would cross the distance between them, the same as they had eaten the speckled toadstools to take them to the mortal realm without fear.

"Louise," he said. He would, a certain man, in place of an uncertain boy.

A smile crept across her face, as warm and inviting as a flower blooming for the sun. "Sacha," Louise whispered. "My Sacha. You're here with me now, aren't you?"

"I am, Louise. I am."

Sweet Latin Prince

D. K. Kayn

I honestly didn't know a lot about the Arracian Royal Family. I knew they were the only royal family in the Americas, but I didn't even realize that up until about two years ago. The Kingdom of Arracia wasn't really on the U.S. military's list of countries of concern. It was, after all, a constitutional monarchy, like the United Kingdom or Japan. The closest I'd ever been to Arracia was Jamaica, its neighbor to the northeast. Though I'd never visited Arracia, I imagined it to be blazing hot with a powerful sun like its Caribbean neighbors and Central America to the west.

When I arrived on the island, it was as hot as I thought it'd be. The blue skies were cloudless, so the palm trees above were the only reprieve from the overbearing Caribbean sun. I had to report to the naval base nearby for briefing. It may not have been military-related, but it was government-related, and security clearance was required.

Although the U.S. military base was just a few miles south of San Radaime, the Arracian capital and largest city in the island nation, it was referred to as Naval Station San Radaime. The Arracian Royal Family signed an agreement with the president of the United States so that they could hire bodyguards trained by the U.S. military for each member.

"Your assignment is to Prince Hector," the detailer, Mr. Ryan Daley, told me.

When he set the prince's picture before me, I was a bit taken aback. It was a picture of him smiling and dressed in a business suit, the same as almost all royals I'd seen. He wasn't as young as I thought, and was probably somewhere around my age. I was initially picturing a child. His olive-toned skin and black hair were obvious markers of his mixed Spanish and Amerindian heritage, like many Arracians. His face was lightly coated in a thin layer of scruff, and a smile crinkled the skin around his brown eyes. He was … *gorgeous*, and an obvious chick magnet.

Prince Hector Quesada, just called Prince Hector, was twenty-six—one year younger than me—and was the eldest of three. He resided in the Royal Palace of San Radaime with the rest of the royal family. I imagined this guy had to be a millennial marketing goldmine. He was young, attractive, and literally a prince. What could go wrong?

❦

San Radaime reminded me of Spain, as it should've, since Arracia was one of its colonies up until the early 1800s. The Spanish influence was almost unerasable, though the nation's Caribbean flair was powerful.

The city wound about the royal palace, almost as if it was built around it. When we pulled up to the gates decorated with the letters *S* and *R* on either side, the gate guard inspected the vehicle before letting us through. There was security all around. All were armed and vigilant.

The palace's baroque architecture was another definite testament to the nation's Spanish influence. It was enormous, wider than any building I'd seen. It almost looked like a widespread Catholic church from the outside. The interior was almost exclusively marble laced with gold. Gargantuan statues lined the atrium, and nineteenth-century Arracian art hung about the walls. From a distance, I could see a hall with paintings of men and women in crowns—the past kings and queens of Arracia, I assumed. A group of tourists was in that area.

I laughed to myself, thinking that I could never live in a place where so many people could tour and move in and out of. Then again, I *was* living here for the next few weeks.

We ascended to the second floor, which was off-limits to tourists and unauthorized personnel. The third floor was the start of the living quarters.

"Okay, wait here, and I will return," my escort, Mr. Montoya, said to me before disappearing out of the doorway of the room to which he led me. Montoya was a sort of liaison between the Royal Service and the U.S. military. He worked and lived in the palace.

I put down my bags for a moment and poked around the room. It was an office of sorts. It seemed that it hadn't been an office for a while, though, as there were no papers, writing utensils, or office supplies of any sort. There were paintings on the wall, but I could not immediately decipher any of the faces. I wondered if the prince would prefer I speak to him in Spanish or English. Both were major languages in the nation, with Spanish being the official language.

Then the door opened behind me. My heart fluttered for a moment. *Damn*, I thought. *He really is attractive.*

"Your Highness, this is Marcus Harrington," said Montoya. "He'll be your bodyguard."

There he stood, face still adorned with a slight scruff. He smiled, but it wasn't like the smile in the photo. His face looked a bit different; it seemed a bit colder, less inviting. I didn't make a face or react. Montoya continued his introduction.

"Mr. Harrington, this is Prince Hector," he said.

The prince didn't meet my gaze as I stared at him, searching for a reaction. A thought tumbled into the back of my mind that maybe he had something against black people. I didn't let the thought flourish because, either way, he was stuck with me. Even if he had prejudices, I was being paid to live in this palace and protect him. It was my job to keep him alive, not accommodate any possible prejudices he may have.

Spoiled little shit, I thought. I extended my hand out of habit, unaware if I should bow or curtsy or whatever the hell people do when royalty is around. Even if I was wrong, I didn't correct myself. He was a man, I was a man, and we could shake hands like men.

The prince extended his hand in return, only meeting my gaze for a moment, but gripping my hand firmly.

Wait, I thought. *Is he … blushing?*

⸎⸎⸎

By day six, the prince has barely said a word to me. He did look at me once, but the moment he did, I caught him, and he looked away. I wasn't quite sure how to deal with that.

Every day, I'd stand outside his bedroom door as he showered to ensure he wasn't bothered. He'd told me he didn't prefer it, but it was an order from the king. On this particular day, he was taking a much longer time than usual. Over the past few days, he would emerge from his room approximately ten minutes after the shower had stopped. It had now been thirty minutes. A press conference in the atrium below was underway, and they were waiting for Prince Hector.

Paranoia set in. I knocked on the door and waited. No answer. What the hell was he doing in there? I thought something could be wrong. My paranoia got the best of me, and I went in without a second thought. The moment I opened the door, I immediately wished I hadn't.

He had his back to the door, preoccupied with something on the table in front of him. He wasn't wearing anything, revealing his chiseled back muscles leading down to his obscenely large glutes. The prince wasn't a big guy by any means, but his ass was a sight to behold. It wasn't as muscled as the rest of him, and he had thick thighs to match. I didn't need a view from the side to see how thick and round it was, a perfect semicircle curving out from his sternum. Arracia was a country known for sexy men and women with big butts. Even the crown prince fell within those bounds.

Fuck, I thought, swiftly shutting the door behind me. I closed my eyes in an attempt to blink away what I'd seen, but it only photographed the image, burning it into my mind. I was rock hard.

He was dressed approximately ten minutes after I'd peeked. *Why the hell did I have to do that?* I thought.

When he emerged from his room, he smiled at me, signaling that he was ready to go. I smiled back, covering my erection. I hadn't even noticed his ass before; the blazer of every suit he'd worn managed to cover it up.

✧◦•◦✧

Day twelve of duty was dull as ever. I was restless and needed to get laid badly. When no one was around, I ended up Googling "Arracian prince ass," and found numerous results. Apparently, the Arracian prince's ass was world-renowned. I searched images that highlighted it, and then I came across the one. Prince Hector was in a business suit, walking up a flight of stairs. The wind had caught him at the right angle and blew the back of his blazer upward, revealing the perfect arc of his ass. The picture was captioned, "The Prince and His Bubble Butt."

Boy, were they right. If only they'd seen what I'd seen. *No, no, no,* I thought. I should think about something else. This type of lust was going to distract me from my job. I thought back to an old roommate I had on active duty named Jarret Bridges. He preferred I called him by first name, and I told him he could call me by mine.

I remember one day after I finished work, I came back to my barracks room, where Jarret was doing a few exercises post-workout. Jarret's pale arms reddened with strain as he forced out one last push-up. He held his position at the lean and rest, no doubt taking a small break before taking on his next exercise.

I sat on my bed, squirming anxiously and trying to pay attention to my television instead of Jarret. I always hated watching him workout. Even after ten months of living with and seeing the same guy, I still was not accustomed to watching him. I would normally have been able to contain my eyes, forcing them into occupation with anything else in the room. That day, however, the sound of Jarret's grunts and heavy breathing frustrated me, causing me to squirm even more. I knew I should've looked at anything but Jarret, but I decided to torture myself for the millionth time.

Jarret remained in the push-up position, still huffing. The perfect bulge of his triceps remained hardened and tense as his arms kept him elevated. His perfectly chiseled back glittered with sweat, leading down to his perfectly rounded, thick ass, concealed by gray basketball shorts that were tight enough to highlight the roundness of each cheek.

I bit my lip. *This isn't fair*, I'd thought to myself. *Thousands of Marines and I get roomed with this one.* I'd joined the military to earn money for school, and because I'd hated living with my parents. The Navy hadn't been all I had hoped for, but anything was better than living with them.

Jarret finally stood, grabbing a towel to dry the sweat from his body. He walked into the bathroom and closed the door behind him. I'd immediately pulled my pants down and began stroking quickly. I wouldn't have been able to wait until later that night. I thought about the things I would do to Jarret's perfect ass if he would let me. I'd imagined the lubricated hole my hand made as Jarret's tight, thick anus that fit my dick like a glove. I licked my lips at the thought of what his hole might taste like. My mouth watered like a dog salivating over a thick, juicy steak.

I'd imagined Jarret's thick cheeks on top of my face, my tongue sliding up and down Jarret's clean, moistened hole. I could almost taste it. Then my nut shot up to my chest in thick, greedy bursts as my dick throbbed, pumping as much of it out as possible. I opened my eyes to see the mess I'd made, then I looked to the open bathroom door, where Jarret stood staring at me, eyes bulging as I lay on my bed with my dick in my hand and a mess of cum all over my chest and stomach.

Jarret and I never spoke of the instance again. Then we both deployed in our separate units and never saw each other after.

I closed my eyes and stroked, picturing Jarret's round, naked cheeks. I was lying to myself. Jarret wasn't gay or bi; he was a straight dude. Besides, that was years ago. I thought about the prince's ass again. I didn't have to use my imagination too much since I'd already seen his naked cheeks. *Goddamn*, I thought.

Prince Hector had just showered when I saw him naked. He smelled amazing when he'd stepped out of the door. I wanted to catch the first whiff of him as he hopped out of the shower, to watch the leftover water glisten against his olive skin. I imagined the water sliding between those massive cheeks of his. In my mind, they weren't firm. They were soft, jiggling with his every movement. I wanted to be under them. I wanted to lay down on the floor as he lowered his ass to my face.

I licked my lips, salivating at the thought of the taste of him. I stroked harder, feeling myself lose it before a knock came to the door. I grumbled, pulled up my pants, and answered the door. When I opened it up, I didn't expect to see Prince Hector staring back at me.

"Hi," he said.

"Your Highness," I said as a greeting. I almost asked him, "What the hell do you want?" as if I wasn't just touching myself while thinking about him and looking at a candid picture of his bubble butt in a suit. He wore casual clothes now.

Damn it, I thought. He was so sexy it was insane. He could make a simple pair of jeans and a T-shirt look damn good. He smelled amazing, like he'd prepared himself to go someplace.

"I need you to take me somewhere," he said, as if it wasn't nearly ten o'clock at night.

I took note of the fact that this wasn't a request. "Shouldn't you let Mr. Montoya—"

"I've already let him know," he said, interrupting me.

"Of course, sir," I said, gritting my teeth.

❦

When we arrived at the nightclub, I was nervous. I was literally carrying royalty in the backseat, and he wanted to waltz into this place as though he wasn't. He asked me to pull around to the back of the club. Some men dressed in dark clothing were waiting at the back door as we pulled up. Bouncers, I guessed.

"Just wait for me back here, and I'll be back shortly," said Prince Hector.

"Your Highness, are you sure about—"

"I said, I'll be back shortly," he said firmly, cutting me off and getting out of the car promptly.

I felt my heart pump, and the hairs on the back of my neck stand up. He really just cut me off. If this wasn't my job, I'd have told him off, but I reminded myself that this was just that—my job. I watched him stroll off into the back door of the club, greeting the men on his way in as if there had been some form of camaraderie that existed long before mine with the prince.

I killed the engine, pulled out my phone, and casually searched for El Jefé, the name of the place we'd arrived at. I didn't know any clubs in this country. El Jefé was rated four-and-a-half stars when I searched it. A review written in Spanish said something about it being the best club on the island. I allowed myself to rest on the thought that this was just a bit of innocent fun and that he just wanted to have a bit of normality in his abnormal life. I ended up browsing the web for no good reason before I realized nearly half an hour had passed.

I got a text from Mr. Daley.

Hey, I got a message from Montoya. Where are you?

Oh boy. It'd sound pretty bad if I told him I'd let the prince out of my sight, especially in a nightclub. Where the hell was he?

Prince Hector needed to step out for a minute. What's the problem?

The problem is that Montoya went to the prince's room, his door was wide open, and Montoya was told that he was nowhere to be found.

I sighed. I should've known better. He hadn't told Montoya that he was stepping out.

You serious? He's here with me. Get him home ASAP.

Shit. I put my phone away and went to the back door of the club. I knocked on the door but got no response. I was sure they couldn't hear anything over the music. I knocked harder. Still nothing. I hurried to the front of the club, where a bouncer stood at the door, halting my path.

"I need to get in," I said.

The bouncer just looked at me. He was a burly man with a goatee and long, black hair he tied into a ponytail.

I pulled out my ID. "I'm with the Royal Service."

At that, he moved away from the door with a huff of annoyance. "You got any weapons?" he asked.

"No," I said.

He still used his metal detector anyway, finding nothing on me.

Inside, the music boomed with whatever this latest reggaeton hit was. At the DJ booth, a big man in a New York Knicks jersey spun records, while countless people danced like there was a ton of room in this place. As I made my way through the crowd, searching every face for the prince, I could feel sweat creeping down my back. I was going to need a shower after leaving this place. Then I saw a man in a familiar T-shirt and pair of jeans wearing a jester's mask … the prince.

He was dancing in a way that almost seemed out of character for him. He jumped and waved his arms around. I actually wondered if I had the wrong guy for a moment. I tapped him on the shoulder, and he turned to me. I pressed my mouth to his ear.

"We need to go," I said.

"I told you I would come back!" he yelled. "Now go back to the car!"

I looked at him, searching his face for a sign that he wasn't serious. He turned away from me. He was serious. That had been the third time tonight he'd spoken to me in a way I didn't appreciate, no matter if he was a prince.

I wrapped my arms around his torso with his arms pressed to his sides, and he writhed in my grip. I was already prepared for the inevitable struggle. With him lifted, we made our way through the crowd that parted as he bucked in my arms, his perfect ass pressed uncomfortably against my waist. I made my way to the back exit, pleading for it to lead me to the alleyway. It did. When we exited the club, a rush of fresh air filled my lungs. I dropped him, and he used the car to stop himself from falling over.

"What the hell?" he exclaimed. "I could have you fired for embarrassing me like this!"

"My job is to protect you," I said, feeling myself snap. "If you think lying to me is going to be part of my job, you've got it all wrong."

He didn't say another word; he just looked at me. The fury in his gaze died a bit. He looked like he almost felt guilty for a moment, but then he scowled again.

"Now get in the car," I said. "I'm taking you home."

It took me a while to stop reeling from the fact that I'd just spoken to royalty this way. Me, a black dude from Virginia, was barking orders at a Caribbean prince. Hector didn't speak on the ride back.

When we arrived, Montoya was upset. I explained the situation to him, but he didn't want to hear it. The prince didn't speak to me for a couple more days. Press conferences went by in a blur.

I started to feel guilty. This was all his life had been about. Prince Hector had no other outlets besides occasionally sneaking into a party or two just to feel like a normal human being. Honestly, I couldn't relate. I grew up in a broke family in Norfolk, Virginia. I joined the military to change my life, and it led me here. So many people I knew, and even I, at one point, would've given anything to be in Prince Hector's shoes.

The night before my transfer, I looked out of my window, watching the palm trees sway in the night breeze and the Caribbean Sea beat against the shores. I had spent a month in the palace. Then a knock came to my door. It was Prince Hector.

"May I come in?" he asked abruptly. It was the most polite thing he'd said to me in all my time here.

I moved from the doorway, allowing him to enter. He shut the door behind him. I froze for a moment, wondering what he could've wanted that the door couldn't stay open for.

He sighed.

"Something you wanted to talk about, Your Highness?" I asked, urging him on.

He sighed again before speaking. "No one's ever spoken to me the way you did," he said.

My face twisted in confusion at first. I remembered Montoya but then ruled him out, as most of his anger that night had been directed at me.

"None of the bodyguards I've had have shown that much of an interest in my safety." He paused again.

I went to open my mouth to speak but was sharply cut off.

"I wanted to apologize for the way I've been toward you," he said. "It was inappropriate and rude. I'm sorry."

I couldn't believe it. A prince had given me an apology. Was he shaken by the fact that I put him in his place?

"Wow, um … thank you, Your High—"

"Hector," he said. "Just Hector."

He held out his hand to shake mine; I took it firmly. He stared at me a long moment, and I stared back, gazing into those deep brown eyes. I observed every feature of his face, his trimmed beard, his luscious lips. We gazed at one another for so long that we hadn't realized we were still holding one another's hands. Hector moved closer to me, still holding my hand. I didn't move; I was frozen in place. He was right in front of me, so close I could smell his cologne. I gulped.

He let go of my hand and took my wrist, slowly moving it to his back. *Are you serious?* I wanted to ask. I felt for the small of his back, playing it cool. He pulled me closer to him. Our lips were close. I could feel his breath against mine, intermingling there for a sweet moment.

"It's okay," he said, pulling me even closer to him.

Then our lips smashed into each other's. It was gentle at first, but then it grew more animalistic. This was primal. This was truly what I had been dying for, I knew it. This prince. My prince.

He pulled away for a moment, breathing a sigh and resting my forehead against his. "It's okay," he said again, using his hand to lower my wrist so that my right hand could reach his left ass cheek.

I cupped it in my hand, gently at first, feeling the weight of the cheek in my hand. I was right; it wasn't firm. It was soft, *so* soft, and plushy, yet meaty. This ass wasn't the result of endless glute exercises; this guy was blessed with this ass.

"Squeeze it," he whispered. "Squeeze hard."

I did, cupping the cheek harder. He sucked in a gasp and released a moan in response, resting his forehead against my shoulder. *God, don't let this be a dream*, I begged. *If it is a dream, please don't wake me up.*

I grabbed the other cheek with my opposite hand, squeezing both cheeks with most of the strength in my hands. Hector moaned again, digging his head into my shoulder. He returned his lips to mine, taking control of my mouth and my tongue. I held firmly to his ass while we kissed, backing him into a wall.

"Fuck," he sighed, attempting to catch his breath.

My thoughts exactly, I wanted to say.

Hector took off his shirt in a hurry. I was wrong about him being muscular. He was toned, but not musclebound. There were obvious signs that he frequented the gym, as the tone of his arms and chest showed. His stomach was flat, not chiseled with a six-pack, but toned like the rest of him.

"I'm clean … you know … back there," he said.

That did it. Like a maniac, I nearly threw him to the bed. I turned him over and almost ripped the loose basketball shorts from his body. When he was free of all clothing, I stood there, staring at the round, beautiful cheeks in front of me. I grabbed each cheek, squeezing hard and listening to Hector moan before I even had time to do anything. I raised and dropped a forceful palm against his right cheek. The sound echoed off the walls.

"Oh, my God!" he exclaimed, his mouth agape and eyes closed.

Then I moved in, spreading his cheeks apart. I inhaled the sweet scent of oils he'd applied after cleaning. He really prepared for this. Maybe he didn't know this would happen, but he was hoping for it just as much as I was. *Goddamn it*, I thought. This man was so sexy. This prince. This spoiled, sexy prince.

I pressed my whole mouth to his anus, kissing and sucking like I had his tongue just earlier. Muffled moans came from the head of the bed. Hector had stuffed his face into a pillow. He squirmed as I licked and sucked on his sweet asshole. He'd prepared his ass just for me like a delicious evening dinner. My dick throbbed, and my shorts were soaked in precum. I flattened my tongue and gave his anus several long licks. I opened my eyes and looked over his meaty mounds to his smooth back as he squirmed and gave moans of pleasure.

I peeled off my shorts and my wet boxer briefs, freeing my dick. I stood up from my kneeling position. Hector turned back to me.

"Shit," he said in a gasp, observing my erection. "It's so big."

His eyes were practically bulging from their sockets as though he'd never seen a dick as big as mine. I liked that thought. I wanted to think that I was the biggest he'd ever had and that I would be an experience to remember. I stroked myself over him.

He sat up on the bed with his lips right near my dick. I could see him visibly shudder at the sight of it. He looked up at me. There was a reverence in his gaze like he was worshipping me. He consumed me with his eyes like he couldn't get enough of me. I got even harder than I thought possible; it was almost physically painful. I held my dick in my hand as precum dripped from the tip of it. Hector opened as I guided it into his warm mouth. I threw my head back in pleasure.

He bobbed back and forth, slowly at first, coming into a rhythm. Once he caught a good pace, it was like he'd gotten even hungrier. He sucked me like it was his only form of sustenance, like I would vanish if he didn't suck me in enough time. He occasionally paused, either to catch his breath or to let the tip of my dick tickle the soft spot at the back of his throat. This prince was no amateur.

I could feel myself losing it; I would have come if he hadn't stopped. He stood up and immediately pressed his lips to mine. I kissed him back, neither of us caring where on each other's bodies our mouths had been. I grabbed his ass again, squeezing both thick cheeks as I drew him against me, feeling his erection press against mine. It was almost like it wasn't enough, like I couldn't get closer.

I picked him up again, not throwing him to the bed like before, but placing him down gently. We continued to kiss, then I slipped my hand over to my nightstand and retrieved the lube and condoms. I drew back, allowing him to see what I had in my hand. My heart raced a bit at the thought that he might reject this, that he wouldn't want it. He reached for my hand, removed the condom, and put it back into the drawer. He took both sides of my face and pulled me down as if to kiss me, but he dodged my mouth and whispered in my ear.

"I want to feel you," he said.

I shuddered, fighting back an embarrassing whimper. I uncapped the lube and gave myself a good few strokes, careful not to give too many. Hector lubed his hole nice and good, teasing it with his middle fingers to loosen himself up. He wrapped his arms around me as I went in, giving a squeal and whimper as I entered. I nearly did the same and went in as far as I could, awaiting his approval as I moved incrementally.

I gave slow thrusts that eventually became stronger piston movements. I looked into those sweet brown eyes, nearly lost in them. Hector wrapped his legs around me as if begging me not to leave. I didn't want to leave, and I didn't want to finish, but I couldn't hold it any longer. I went in for a few more strokes and was nearly there.

"Come in me," said Hector. One of his hands stroked his own dick while the other gripped my arm.

I came, my dick pulsing in heated spurts as I emptied my load into him. He moaned, shooting onto his own chest and stomach. Both of us gasped for breath. I hung my head as he covered his eyes with his free arm. I felt a bubble of laughter build in my stomach. I'd never been so satisfied. He uncovered his face, and we looked into each other's eyes briefly before sharing another hungry kiss.

❧❧❧

After we cleaned ourselves off, we lay next to one another, talking. This was the most Hector had spoken to me my entire time here. He told me he liked men. He'd had sex with a few men, but he had to sneak since it was not something his father would approve of.

"Do you like women?" I asked.

Hector hesitated, shifting uncomfortably. "No," he said. "Do you?"

"Not as much as guys," I answered honestly. There were a few women I'd found appealing but not nearly as many as men I found appealing. "Is that okay?"

"Yeah, of course," he said. "As long as you're into me, that's all that matters." He pulled me closer, stealing a kiss.

"You don't have to worry about that," I said. "I wish you had told me this weeks ago."

"Better late than never, right?"

Late wasn't as good. I wanted him. I wanted more of this, but I would be leaving. The sad reality dawned on me that he was, after all, royalty, and I was a sailor from the United States. We lived in two different worlds.

"You'll come back to visit."

I noticed his tone again, that tone that told me this wasn't a request or a question. "How would I do that?" I asked. "I don't have money to spare like that."

Hector furrowed his brows at me. "Who said anything about you paying? Did you forget I'm a prince?"

I smiled at him. *No, I didn't*, I thought. I would never forget this sweet prince. I would remember this night for years to come, and every sweet night we would spend together after. Even if it was years down the line, I would always want him. We interlocked our fingers, and I kissed his sweet lips.

"I could never forget that," I said.

The Impossible Lovers

E. W. Farnsworth

Shoula, who loved mathematics, sat with her friend in the atrium of their California community college doing figures. They were used to dealing with harsh, desert sunlight from their native Iraq. Sunblock and sunglasses helped shield them, but the key to survival was water. Shoula had taken the last sip of her bottled water, and she wanted another bottle.

At the next table was a handsome young man named Reza, an Iranian who had taken a fancy for Shoula though they had never been properly introduced. He saw what the girl needed and stood to offer his services. "If you want another bottle of water, I'll get one for you. I was just going to fetch one for myself."

Preoccupied, the girl shook her head, but upon seeing the earnest look in the man's eyes said, "You may if you also bring one for my friend." She gestured toward Maya, who blushed and looked down.

Reza sprang toward the concession stand and came back with three bottles dripping with condensation. He handed one bottle to each of the women and kept the other for himself. Emboldened by his success, he was about to strike up a conversation when two burly men came out of nowhere to stand on either side of Shoula with their arms folded.

"Don't mind them. My father insists on bodyguards. They make sure I'm not threatened."

The two men were now looking over the two bottles to be sure their seals had not been broken. Satisfied, they put the bottles down again and stepped back before they retired to their table nearby. The bodyguards' eyes never left the young women.

The young benefactor shrugged and chuckled. Shoula thought he had an impish expression. She saw that he was not the least intimidated by her protectors.

"I'm glad to see you are well guarded. These are violent times. In fact, I have bodyguards too, only they don't watch so close up as yours."

"Pardon me, but do you do cube roots?" She was now looking over her glasses into his eyes.

Without blinking, he nodded. "Try me."

"Seven hundred twenty-nine," she said. "That should be easy."

"Nine!" He unscrewed his bottle top and took a long draft.

She rattled off several long numbers that were not exact cubes, and he had no trouble rattling off the solutions. Then he fired back a very long sequence of numbers, and she instantly delivered the cube root.

"That's correct. So you've proven that you are as good as a pocket calculator."

She smiled. "My father used to brag that I was the modern-day Hypatia."

"Good for you. We need more mathematicians. Are you studying to be an engineer?"

She laughed. "Nothing that practical, though it's always a fallback."

"What's your major?"

"I'm majoring in art. We both are. I am Shoula. Please meet Alia. She has been my friend since Baghdad. We are inseparable."

"Are you related? There's something similar about your eyes."

"We're both Hashemites."

He bowed slightly to both women and said, "I am Reza. I am also studying something impractical—Persian poetry. My professor had to get special authorization for me to do tutorials with him."

"You look Iranian. Do you speak Farsi?"

"I am what you might term 'the genuine article,' and I do speak Farsi. I also write poetry." He pointed toward a well-thumbed notebook. "I'm looking for a publisher."

Shoula thought for a while. She liked his being an aspiring poet. She had dabbled in Farsi, but her father had disapproved. This young man was everything her father had warned her about. Her companion was frowning behind her shades. The mathematician took her own notebook out of her lap and placed it on the table.

"I have a notebook too, only mine is full of tiles."

"Tiles?"

"Did you know that two tiles were only discovered recently? I am struggling to find others that no one has found before. It's fun looking for things that are right in front of you and have not been seen yet."

"I write poetry on that theme. Some Persian art has animals hidden in tracery patterns. Only the adept can find the animals."

"It seems cruel that our Islamic religion forbids human figures in art."

He shook his head. "I don't think so. Are you aware that there is a Muslim Kama Sutra?"

Shoula held her hand over her mouth to hide her smile. Her friend did the same. "My father warned me about that book. He claimed it was full of lies and deceptions, particularly in its descriptions of positions." She shook her head slightly as she returned to her math scribbles.

"Should I ask you out to dinner? Or should I ask your friend to ask you? Or should I ask you both to dinner? What is your protocol?"

Shoula looked at him over her glasses. Her eyes, she hoped, looked friendly but not *too* friendly. Her mind was doing calculations about his question. She thought, *This young man Reza seems to be a gentleman, but who can tell these days?*

"Why don't we three have a feast of lamb and invite our bodyguards?"

"I'd like that. Where shall we find the lamb?"

"It is already hanging in my room. My bodyguards will roast the meat, and we will all share it. I'll make yogurt, and we'll have Medjool dates and ripe green figs. For dessert, we'll have shaved ices." She saw how Reza licked his lips, anticipating the tastes as she listed the foods.

"When will this feast be served?"

"Tonight, of course. Why wait? The lamb has aged. Alia and I will drop by the market. Does seven o'clock tonight sound all right?"

The women were picking up their things and standing up to leave. They had lifted their waters yet untouched. The two bodyguards had risen also.

Reza stood to say goodbye. "Where shall I meet you?"

"Come back here to the atrium at six-thirty. One of my bodyguards will be here to lead you to the feast." Shoula led the way, and in her train came Alia and the two bodyguards.

Reza watched them depart. Shoula turned back to see him before she passed out of sight. She knew he could not see her eyes, but he was clearly smitten. She was already plotting how to manage this lovesick deer when she felt a tugging at her sleeve.

"Shoula, should we be doing this? A feast? We've only just met him."

"Nothing ventured, Alia, nothing gained. You can complain to my father, but by the time he reads your letter, the evening will be over, and we'll have moved to other, more important things."

Alia was not amused. She mumbled to herself as they did their shopping. By the time they arrived at their rooms, they had everything they needed for their feast. Shoula gave instructions to her bodyguards. Then she napped for an hour before she prepared the meal. By then, one bodyguard had lighted coals in a brazier. She and Alia chopped lamb, vegetables, and fruits to be speared as shish kebab. Alia stirred saffron into the steamed rice while Shoula set out the fruits and yogurt.

The guests began to arrive at a quarter to seven. Twelve guests, including the bodyguards, were expected. Reza arrived to find a medium-sized dinner party in progress. The gathering was informal but included poets, singers, musicians, dancers, and artists from all over the Middle East. Shoula smiled when she announced that Reza would recite some of his original poetry. He did not appear the least surprised. He inspected the roasting kebabs and arranged a plate with an assortment of flatbreads and dips.

Each guest at the party was introduced by one of Shoula's bodyguards. He or she would then demonstrate by playing, singing, dancing, reciting, and the like. So they provided their own entertainment while they feasted.

Shoula was pleased to have the group come together at her place. She explained to Reza that theirs was a moveable feast. "You never can guess where we'll be meeting next. Of course, that's partly for security. Speaking of which, the bodyguard who brought you here identified your two protectors in the shadows. If you like, you can invite them to the feast. There's plenty to go around."

Reza stepped outside and beckoned for his people to enter. They were reluctant at first, but they came and ate. They also recited poetry in their own languages.

"You have a literary entourage!"

"We do like sharing poetry. I managed to have my bodyguards' works published in Iran. Unfortunately, the ayatollahs objected to the content of those works, and they were banned."

"I'll bet they were racy."

"Not so much, no. The ayatollahs will object to anyone associated with me on political grounds."

Shoula nodded. "I know what that's like. Will you have tea?"

She poured him tea and invited him to sample her spice seeds and pastries.

The feasting continued until ten o'clock, and Shoula stood by the door to bid everyone goodbye. Reza lingered until only Shoula, Alia, and he remained.

"I very much enjoyed the feast. I had no idea you had such a salon going. It is a lot like the underground culture in my country. Since my uncle, the shah, was overthrown, the arts and literature have suffered. No one knows when things will change, but when they do change, I will go back and try to set things right."

"Are you in the line of succession?"

"Yes, but others stand before me."

"I can understand that too. Goodnight. Come again. Next time, bring your bodyguards right in. There's no sense leaving them outside hungry and in the dark."

Shoula closed the door when he had left. She helped Alia clean up. By eleven o'clock, she was deep into her homework problems. She found the balance of math and designs refreshing. As she thought about the evening, she kept dwelling on Reza with his mellifluous voice reciting poetry and on Reza laughing with his mustache wiggling beneath his nose.

The Iranian prince became a regular at Shoula's dinner parties. It was clear to her and everyone else that the young man was becoming devoted to her. She refused to acknowledge his growing affection to anyone but Alia, her father's faithful spy.

"Shoula, don't you think you should cut off Reza before it is too late?"

"Ridiculous, Alia. There's no harm in the man. He's a Shi'ite, and I am Sunni. So what?"

"He is a prince, and you are a princess. This is a matter of state, after all."

"Nonsense. His claim to royalty is tangential. You know how far from the throne I happen to sit. The chances of our both ending up on the respective thrones of Iraq and Iran are nil. So relax. Do some more work on your painting. I like its blues and greens."

Alia shook her head in disapproval about Shoula's relationship with the Persian, but she liked her mistress's approval of her art. She was preparing for her one-person show at the college gallery. It was scheduled to appear the last month of the semester, just after Shoula's one-person show.

Shoula finished the twentieth piece for her show, and she decided to throw a pre-show dinner party at which she would exhibit her artwork on her own apartment walls. She made individual invitations to this "rehearsal" for her big show.

Reza was particularly laudatory. "I liked receiving your invitation. I hope you don't mind, but I wrote a small poem in honor of your exhibit." He handed her the copy and a translation. She read through the piece and smiled.

"Thank you. The sentiment is beautifully expressed. With your permission, I'm going to post your poem at the entrance to the gallery."

"I have no objection. Will you have dinner with me after your opening reception?"

Shoula realized this was several moves ahead of where she intended to be with this young man, but she had no objection, and she reasoned that she could handle Alia's negativism. As for her father's wrath, that was another matter. She and Reza had not reached a crucial moment in their relationship. She thought, *What harm could possibly come from our sharing a meal?*

The pre-opening and the opening went well. Over two hundred faculty members, administrators, and students attended Shoula's exhibition.

At their private dinner afterward, Reza was all praise. "Shoula, you have been a marvelous success. I saw the critic for the city newspaper walk through making copious notes. His photographer was taking pictures. Thank you again for posting my poem at the entrance. I received a couple of nice comments."

"Reza, you should think of holding a one-person recitation of your latest. Maybe that could be part of Alia's show. We'll have to ask her."

"She hates me. I don't know why, but she entirely disapproves of my spending time with you. She must be fit to be tied tonight."

"She's not, really. That's because she doesn't know we're together."

Reza's jaw dropped. "But your bodyguards are still watching you. In fact, they're at the small table around the pillar over there." He pointed in their direction, and they waved at him in return.

"They won't ever take their eyes off me, but Alia is another matter. She and they have orders to report my activities to my father, but I have a deal with my bodyguards."

"You pose a mystery. I sense an opportunity."

"Reza, you scoundrel!" She was smiling as she contemplated the mischief they might do by the rules of her father's game.

The Iranian had a sheepish smile. "I may be a scoundrel, but I have fallen in love with you, and I'd like you to tell me what we're going to do about that." He sipped his drink and looked around for his own bodyguards.

"Yes, and we'll have to find ways of circumventing your own security men too."

As he walked her back to her apartment, Reza was careful to ensure that both squads of watchers could keep them in view. He took her hand at her door and kissed it lightly. This pleased her, and she blushed. Then she ducked right up to his face and kissed him on the lips. He kissed her back and held her for a moment in his arms.

Breaking free for a breath of air, he said, "This will be continued soon—at least, I hope so. Just nod once, and I shall be the happiest man alive."

She did that just before Alia pulled open the door with a disapproving scowl. "I'm glad you decided to return before I called the police to have all the rivers dragged. Wait until your father reads about your wandering off with a male companion—and without me!"

Shoula said, "Go stuff it somewhere, Alia. Reza and I had dinner together, but we were being watched the whole time by my bodyguards and his. What could we have possibly done while under that kind of surveillance?"

Alia grabbed her roommate's arm and drew her inside. With her other hand, she slammed the door on Reza's happy face. She immediately opened the door again to utter a cheerful "Get lost!"

Shoula did a pirouette and went to do her homework problems. She was now plotting how she and Reza could circumvent their security teams and explore their sexuality. Her mind reeled in her meditations, and her body wanted only to be mastered by Reza, whom she thought of as her soul mate. As a modern woman, however, she could not bring herself to picture herself married to Reza or anyone else.

Reza continued to attend Shoula's cultural feasts. Other female attendants liked what they saw in him, and some sidled up to Shoula to inquire whether they might exercise their charms on the man. She had to pretend that she had no interest in him. She even encouraged the others to be forward and let him know what they wanted. Behind her raised hand, she would whisper about the Persian's knowledge of Islamic sexual practices.

"He is a master of the Islamic Kama Sutra. He knows all the positions for men and women, and I have heard he is a consummate teacher as well as an ardent student."

"You sound as if you have been his student yourself. Are you certain you won't be angry with me for seducing him?"

The young women who marched off to be schooled in sex by Reza were disappointed because he claimed that his heart belonged exclusively to Shoula, whom he loved to distraction and wanted to marry someday soon.

The more Shoula learned of Reza's devotion to her, the more she desired to possess him, but she was not a fool. The last thing she wanted was to be pregnant and abandoned by a handsome playboy like him. She decided she needed clarification of their relationship. Once more, they dined alone, but were, of course, observed by their security people.

"Reza, it has come to my attention that my girlfriends have been importuning you to have sex with them. If you want to gratify their wishes, go right ahead. Feel free. Take them around the world. Go through the thirty-four positions of male-female congress. Take them to the moon. Give them clouds and rain." She could not continue, for she was weeping.

Reza let her weep. He took her right hand in one of his hands and stroked it gently with the other. "Your so-called girlfriends are silly lightweights. I love only you. As for all the books on love, I would prefer one night with you to all of them put together. Let's make a date to spend a weekend dallying out of sight of our minders. I'll book a penthouse suite at the Holton Hotel. We'll live on room service from Friday night to Monday morning."

Shoula nodded and studied her plate while he elaborated. She looked up when he had finished his pitch, and her demeanor was deadly serious. "I don't want a one-weekend stand. I want a commitment."

"Do you want me to propose marriage to you? I have already done that. All you need is to answer me."

"I don't want a marriage commitment. I am a modern woman. I don't want to be tied down at all, and certainly not in the traditional way. I have a long and productive career ahead of me. What I require is sex—lots of wild, glorious sex—with a partner who loves and respects me enough to let me remain free."

"Tell me how I can convince you that I will be the lover you have dreamt of?"

"You must convince me that you will master me in sex but respect me as an equal in all other things. If you betray me, I shall cut you off, literally as well as physically." She looked at his lap, and her meaning was graphically clear.

"The Penthouse Suite, then, this Friday. It is Room 7001, the top floor. Come by the back staircase, knock twice, then three times, and then twice again. You must be careful not to be followed by Alia or your bodyguards. Is that understood?"

"Perfectly. What about your security?"

"How about I position them in the hotel's lobby? If we run into trouble we cannot handle, they can come up the elevator or the stairs to rescue us."

"What should I bring with me?"

"Lubricants. Lots of them. Four changes of clothing."

"Will you bring condoms and the sex manuals?"

"Your wish is my command."

"Good." She laughed. "Now that we have settled our tryst, let's have a go at dessert while you tell me your sexual history. I want details." She made this last demand while pointing a fork at his genitals. She watched him squirm, but he collected himself and began telling her everything she wanted to know.

By eleven o'clock, her head was spinning from his tales of conquest and embarrassment. She was so swept up in the role of voyeur, she could hardly stand up. She took his arm and walked to the main entrance of her apartment complex, but she went up to her door alone. Naturally, Alia was waiting for her. She was delighted to see her alone.

"Where have you been, Shoula?"

"I've been studying in the carrel alone. Exams are coming up soon. I'll have to sequester myself from everyone I care for until I have mastered all my materials. You of all people know how my father counts on me to do well."

"I also know you, you little minx. If I discover you have been lying to me about studying, I'll write to your father and suggest he beat your bare backside with a switch."

"You have such a vivid way describing punishments, one would almost surmise you had experienced them yourself. Whether you have been bent over someone's knee with your bare buttocks ready for blistering or not, I can promise you the beating of your life if you tell on me. You know I can command that punishment because I am the legitimate princess."

The two young women glared at each other. They had a standoff, but they would resolve nothing that evening. So, they each went to their work and remained focused on that until morning.

Friday came soon, and Shoula made her way to the Penthouse of the Hilton Hotel. She used the back stairwell and gave the secret knock on the penthouse door. Reza answered, and she flew into his arms. The suite was full of freshly-cut flowers. Above the enormous bed was a mirror that fit the whole ceiling. She showed him what she had brought, and he reciprocated. They installed their sex enhancers on either bedside table. He had brought toys that he had not mentioned at their dinner, and she was intrigued but feigned indifference.

They wasted no time. They tore off each other's clothing and leapt naked into the center of the bed. He kissed her all over, but too quickly for her taste. She asked him to go slowly and savor her.

He slowed and used his tongue to explore every curve and crevasse of her body. She then did the same to him. By then, of course, she was wet, and he was rock hard.

They refused to be rushed into coitus, so their hugging and finger foreplay went on for half an hour. Only then was she begging for him to possess her.

He was long and hard, and his enormous penis looked like a scimitar. Yet he disdained to enter her right away. Instead, he reached to his bedside table for the book with the illustrations of the thirty-four positions and suggested that it was time for them to review each before selecting the one they would try.

"Oh, Reza, do you think we'll have time to go through all of these in our weekend?"

"We can try. We can pick up where we leave off some other weekend."

"Some of these are familiar."

"What?"

"Alia and I have sampled some of these ideas. We pretended we were men so that we did not seem entirely clueless in the act."

"Maybe we should invite Alia to join us in bed?"

Shoula balled her fists and beat him on the chest. He fended off her attack and turned her back to him. She bent over, so he took her from behind. She felt him enter her and slide right to the hilt.

"Oh.," she said in surprise as his cock entered her vagina. Then, as he slid all the way home, she said, "Ah."

He moaned and began a slow in-and-out rhythm. She leaned forward so that he slipped out, and she rolled onto her back and spread her legs wide. He saw what she wanted and mounted her from the front. Her pelvis rose as he rammed home again. She moaned and bucked. She felt him touch her core deep inside. Now they moved as one organism until she felt her first orgasm. She trembled uncontrollably and squeezed him with all her might.

His head rose in delight, and he nodded. "Let's come together. I'm almost there."

"Me too. Give me all of you."

"There." He climaxed, and she experienced her second orgasm. It came in waves, and she pushed on his chest as he arched his back to keep his penis inside.

Then he eased out of her and rolled to one side. She was breathless with excitement, already anticipating their next coupling. She ran her hand down his chest and wrapped her fingers around his wet, hard prick. He smiled at her and kissed her on the lips.

That was Reza and Shoula's first lovemaking. As they worked their way through the Muslim love repertoire, they grew accustomed to each other's special needs. Shoula once shouted, "Oh, Alia!" and Reza whispered, "Fatima," but otherwise, they were devoted to each other.

Their cycles of love and sleep and showers brought them to early Monday morning when, reluctantly, they dressed to return to their normal lives. He kissed her at the door, long and tenderly. She melted and was tempted to rush right back to bed, but they both had classes, and she had explaining to do.

Shoula's Monday Islamic History was the only class she shared with Alia, who looked more robust and energized than ever, and she made no invidious accusations. Her girlfriend's eyes were full of the same dreamy reverie as her own. Now Shoula wanted to satisfy her curiosity. *What has Alia been up to in my absence?* At the first opportunity, she broached the subject of the weekend.

"Oh, Shoula, I have been a very bad girl. Maybe I should be spanked hard on my bare bottom."

Shoula was shocked. Her father's trusted spy had transgressed. But how? "Alia, what have you done?"

"Your friend Reza's two bodyguards invited me to go three-in-a-bed with them at the Hilton Hotel. I was reluctant, but they convinced me to go. I have never had such glorious sex in my life. They took me, and I took them. Many times I was sandwiched between those hunks while their hands wandered all over my body."

"I hope you practiced safe sex."

"It was probably not safe enough."

"You have to be kidding."

"Well, a woman knows when a man has impregnated her."

"Do you know which of your lovers made you feel that way?"

Alia shook her head. "I really don't. It's as if I loved them both in equal measure."

"Be practical, girl. You must choose one."

"How am I going to do that?"

"Let me suggest that the one who comes back to you for a second time is the likely culprit—and father of your child."

"I never dreamed that I would be in this situation … in love with two men and pregnant by one of them." Alia wandered off, skipping and smiling as if she had been relieved of all her troubles.

Shoula thought, *Alia never asked about my weekend. She reminded me, though, to use the little stick to be sure I am not pregnant.*

That evening, Reza knocked on Alia's and Shoula's apartment door. Alia answered. When she saw who it was standing there with the flowers, she called over her shoulder for Shoula to come meet the man with the roses.

When Reza had handed the roses to his beloved, he turned to Alia to say, "You made quite a hit with my bodyguards last weekend. Of the two, Rafiq seems to be head-over-heels in love now."

Alia beamed with joy. "I knew right away that he was the man for me."

"Well, now I must go shopping for a new bodyguard."

Shoula asked, "Why is that, Reza?"

"Rafiq told me he has to resign to find a real job to support Alia. By the way, he intends to propose marriage tonight. He'll be here soon. Please don't let on that I spoiled his secret, but I thought you should be prepared."

"Oh, thank you, Reza!" Alia said, and she kissed him on the cheek.

"Keep your face out of the face of my beloved, or I'll scratch your eyes out."

As if awakening from a dream, Alia cocked her had and looked from one to the other. "Inshallah! We'll have a double wedding before the semester is done. Congratulations, you two. Shoula, your father will be so proud."

Shoula was startled by her friend's well-wishing. She wondered what Alia was going to write to her father now that everything had changed. She took Reza's arm and led him out of the building. "We're going to take a walk to let Alia and Rafiq have a moment of privacy."

"I thought you were going to steer me back to our favorite hotel."

"I could do that. In fact, I shall. We have only begun our mutual explorations. Rather than being tired and sore, I am randy and ready for our new start."

"You said you did not want to answer my proposal of marriage."

"That was before. This is now."

"Is that a yes?" He smiled and squeezed her hand.

"It's a definite maybe. We'll see how you do at the hotel. If you're really, really good, I may be ready for yes."

Contributors

Wolfgang Domino

Wolfgang Domino is passionate about writing erotica. He lives in the woods of Maine, enjoys chess, cycling and reading.

Some of his work has appeared on *Myerotica.com* and *Literotica.com*. Wolfgang is currently working on a novella he hopes to finish sometime next year.

Shanjida is an Indie author, and even a Wattpad writer. She first started writing on Wattpad. Then with the love and support of her readers, she self-published her first book, *Destroyed (Dark Love Due#1)*.

Meanwhile, when she is not writing, Shanjida spends her free time reading books or improving her art skills as an Art student. She lives in Bangladesh with her family and completing her studies in English Language and Art.

January Wren is a romance author and dabbles in the horror genre too—though you won't find her sleeping in the dark!. She is an undergraduate student, one that can usually be found with a cat on her lap, and an iced coffee in her hand. She currently resides on the east coast and is glad that writing doesn't require her to be outside, covered in three feet of snow from December through April!

You can read her fanfiction on Archive of Our Own or connect with her via Tumblr (@Januarywren).

D. K. Kayne

D. K. Kayn is an author of many stories who resides in the Midwestern United States.

E. W. Farnsworth is widely published online and in print. His love stories are fraught with irony, and he often matches people with backgrounds and proclivities that do not mesh in traditional ways.

Other Works from Temptation Press

Summer Fling

Kiss & Tell

The Professor

Private Lessons

Choices

This Sub's for You

Intimate Moments

Forbidden

The Boss

Nights in the City

The Match Game

A Note from the Publisher

How to Thank a Contributor

Dear Reader,

Everyone at Temptation Press would like to thank you for reading *Royal Protection: An Erotic Collection*. If you would like to thank a particular contributor, the best way is to leave a review for them. You may do so by leaving one on our Goodreads page, under the title, *Royal Protection*, by using the link below:

http://www.goodreads.com/TemptationPress

and be sure to mention the contributor directly.

Why should you leave a review? Reviews help budding authors build their credibility in the book industry. By posting a review on Goodreads and other review sites, you help other readers find new authors they may wish to follow, and you never know, your review may end up on an author's website one day.

ᘓᘓᘓ·ᘓᘓᘓ

Friend us on Goodreads:
https://www.goodreads.com/TemptationPress

Visit our website:
http://www.TemptationPress.com